A LUST FOR KNOWLEDGE

By
Marian Ray Greeson

ISBN: 1466364556
ISBN 13: 9781466364554

Chapter 1
Meet Meg and Jean

A long hot late summer day was to be followed by a party at 5:00 PM that afternoon to honor two friends on their birthday. Meg and Jean had arrived back at the university about midday yesterday. They had been home for the summer after completing their second year at WCU.

Meg had spent her summer at home in Murphy. She had spent most of her time helping her parents. Her Dad, Jim Turner, had been the Mayor for several years after successfully seeing that his restaurants, The Harvest Inns, were operating at full capacity all across the state.   Meg had three younger siblings, Lily, Catherine and Charles.. They were still in school in grades 11, 8, and 5.

All of Jim's and Mary's children were very attractive. They all resembled their parent's best features. Jim was tall, blonde and blue eyed. Mary was short, slim and a true brunette.

The three girls were all brunettes. Charles was still short but they all thought he'd be tall when he grew up. He was a true blonde with his Dad's blue eyes.

Meg, the eldest daughter was a musically talented young lady with a mind of her own. She had learned to play both piano and flute and could sing beautifully. She had sung in their church choir throughout her teen years.

Meg and Jean had been best friends since third grade. Jean had moved to Murphy with her parents from Florida. She was an only child. Her family had barely gotten settled into their new home when school opened that year. Meg was in her classroom alone before class, when Mr. and Mrs. Buckner brought Jean to meet her new teacher in her new school. Jean was a very dainty blonde with big blue eyes.

Jean's mother asked, " Where is the teacher?"

Meg said, "She will be here in a few minutes." She added, "Is there something I could do for you?"

The Buckner family were impressed by her maturity and willingness to help them. In just moments, Miss Taylor walked in and greeted the family who awaited her coming. While Miss Taylor was welcoming the Buckner's, Jean and Meg were listening politely to the adults while also smiling at each other.

Meg spoke first, "I am Meg Turner. What is your name?"

Jean smilingly answered, "I'm Jean Buckner. Are you in third grade this year?"

"Yes, I am. Are you new in town?"

"Yes, we only arrived yesterday. Daddy's new job is with the city of Murphy. He is a city planner. Mama is a music teacher."

Meg liked music teachers. She asked, "What does she teach?"

"Piano and voice lessons." Jean responded.

Jean's parents called their daughter over to tell her goodby. Jean wanted them to meet her new friend.

She said, "Mama, this is my new friend, Meg."

Both her parents spoke to Meg and thanked her for her friendly greetings. When they turned to go, Meg asked, "Jean, will you come sit next to me?"

That was all it took for two little girls to become best friends. Meg introduced Jean to all her classmates. Jean was right at home from the beginning, thanks to Meg.

The school years that followed were all happy, busy times for the two friends who were also popular with all of the other classmates. They became leaders in class and in extra curricular activities. Both were musical, athletic and studious.

Meg began learning her piano skills from Jean's Mama. Jean had already learned a lot from her. Both Meg and Jean were gifted in music and Jean learned to like sports as much as Meg.

All the rest of their hometown watched two lovely little girls blossom and grow into young womanhood with all the grace and charm that could be extracted from their closeness and their natural affinity for being in leadership positions in class and on the playground.

Their high school years passed rapidly while they studied and held leadership positions in P.E., music, dramatics, sports, and student affairs. Both girls had starred in several plays.

Jean had also been very active in her classes. She loved to present her book reports dramatically before the entire class. When she was on the volley ball court, she could serve, spike and save lots of plays.

Both girls were well loved by their fellow classmates and were welcomed at all social functions at school and at church. Like all of the young ladies, they dated and partied, always with their best behavior.

Their parents had become good friends and enjoyed lots of their daughters school and church activities. The two families shared vacations and many of the same friends. Jean's Daddy had worked as a city planner, and Meg's Daddy had been busy with his restaurants, the Harvest Home, and was the Mayor so he was in the right position to make friends with Jean's Daddy. Their mothers were both active in church and community activities. They had been more like sisters than just friends.

Chapter 2
Ready to Party?

That is why both Jean and Meg had decided to continue their education at WCU where they were preparing for careers in music and drama. Their house was just as they had left it in June, but now it was cluttered with things brought from home. The prospects looked pretty bad for their party that afternoon at five.

Both girls had lived in the same little house for two years just off campus. Settling in again would take some doing before they could even get started on their refreshments and be squeaky clean and neat by five o'clock.

Both girl's bedrooms were almost ready for occupancy but the living room and kitchen would require attention from both of them.

Since their registering had taken up most of their time yesterday afternoon, they now would have to tackle all the rest of the house together.

They had had to get the porch furniture out of their living room where it had been stored for the summer and replace it in its rightful place on the porch. The potted plants brought from home were to decorate their porch. All had been completed outside before they went to bed last night.

Now their new day had dawned. Meg had gone outside to check on their handy work out front. She called to Jean, "What could have happened out here? Everything is everywhere except where it belongs?"

Jean was gathering laundry when she heard Meg calling her. She had put down the laundry and was going to the door when Meg, almost in tears said, "1 was asking, "What do you think happened out here?"

Jean asked again, "What seems to have happened?"

Jean knew something dreadful had happened because Meg was not very coherent.

Jean looked out the front door. The flower pots and porch furniture were all in disarray.

By the time Jean arrived on the porch, Meg was almost in tears. "Who could have been so mean?"

Jean was completely surprised to find such a mess. She said, "I do not know what happened, but I do think we had best get started getting everything put back where it should be. I'll get this laundry started and be right back."

Meg got the water hose and washed the dirt off the furniture and set each piece back in place. When she looked up, Jean was back and ready to help. They had been working to get the flower pots set upright and refilled with the potting soil that was everywhere except in the pots.

Chapter 3
A Helpful New Friend

They both heard someone walking up the driveway. It was a tall good looking young man they didn't recognize.

He stopped walking and asked, "Could I be of help? That work looks too difficult for you two."

Jean spoke first, "We could use some help but we would not have you to get dirty on our account."

Meg said, "Hello. I wouldn't want you to get dirty either. Someone dumped out our planters after we were in bed last night. We do not know who could have been so mean."

The young man was saying, "I don't mind working in dirt and would be very glad to help if you would allow it."

The girls looked at each other, at the mess, and were thinking about all that they had to do before party time this afternoon. Jean accepted his help and Meg started asking about whether or not he was connected in any way with the university.

The fellow said, "I am Jesse Ray. I am just back from Iraq and have just arrived on campus this morning. All of my registration was completed by the registrar while I was still at home. I have been assigned to a dorm and am all ready to begin"

"Where's home?" Meg wanted to know.

"I grew up on a farm in Virginia. That is why I am used to working in dirt and actually, I am quite good at it,"

Jean asked, "Are you going to major in farming here?"

"Oh, no. I am studying anything other than agronomy. I already know all about that. I have already studied it for most of my 23 years."

It was not what the girls were used to, to be listening to a strangers autobiography. They found it highly unusual, but very interesting.

Meg said, "You don't look like any farmer that I have ever seen, you know, bib overalls and plaid shirt."

"When I joined the service, I knew more uniform ways of dressing were all for me. That was true for a time, but I was glad to return to the states, muster out of the army, and get clothes more suitable to my personality."

Meg and Jean looked at each other and smiled. Together, they said, "Yes, you certainly may help if you are still so inclined."

Jesse joined them beside the porch, knelt down beside the pot they had been working on, and began replacing the spilled soil and resetting the plants so adeptly, that he was finished in less than fifteen minutes. The girls showed him where the pots should go. Jesse moved them with apparent ease. When finished, he asked, "What's next?"

Both girls knew exactly what was next, 'making refreshments'. They looked over the handiwork of all three of them and decided all was well with the porch and hoped that would never happen again. Then Meg said, "We have to get into the kitchen and roll our sleeves up to make refreshments for some fifty hungry people."

"I'm a pretty good cook, too. May I help?" Jesse asked.

Jean answered, "No way. You see our kitchen is hardly big enough for the two of us. But we would love to have you return around five to the party."

"Do you mean, as a guest?" Jesse was pleasantly surprised.

"Oh, yes. You have been lots of help and since you are so new here, that will give you an opportunity to meet about fifty more students."

"There will be some guys here, won't there?" Jesse asked.

"Oh, yes. Lots of guys and gals." the girls answered in unison.

Jesse turned toward the street as he accepted their invitation, saying, "I'll see you about five, then."

Chapter 4
Final Preparations

Jean and Meg surveyed their handiwork once more before hurrying indoors to cook. Meg, with her background in the restaurant business, was all set to make two birthday cakes, one for each of the honored guests, Mary Frances and Nan. Too, she would make cupcakes and two kinds of cookies.

Jean had learned a lot of cooking skills at home with her Mom and also at Meg's home with her Mom. She was to make the veggie tray, dips, serve the potato chips and get out the meats for their tray , prepare the fruit for the fruit tray, and on and on.

Jean had started her inside chores by decorating the living room with balloons, and streamers, candles and candies. That done, she got her fruits and veggies out of the refrigerator and went to do her work on the back porch so as not to get into Meg's way. The porch was comfy with soft chairs and lots of shade from the big trees behind their house.

Jean worked steadily and before she realized it, she had run out of fruit and vegetables to peel and slice. She discarded her peels and gathered her finished products. On entering the kitchen, she saw the beautiful cakes, cup cakes and cookies in all their glory, so beautifully decorated that you would have thought there had been three French chefs at work here.

Jean squealed with pleasure, "Meg, it's all so beautifully done. You have even beaten your own record."

Meg said, "You are just joshing me. I didn't even do all the fancy tricks I have learned over the years."

"I just hope my trays and platters will not look too shabby beside such visions." Jean added as she began to get out trays and platters to fill with her luscious offerings. Meg had looked into the living room between chores and found things there in good shape. Now she got out table clothes to cover the dining table, the sideboard and the various tables they had borrowed from elsewhere in the house.

She began covering the furniture with her baked goods. Jean followed with her fresh items. Jean had made a center piece with fruits and vegetables that was quite unique. She had used a stalk of celery, in the center that stood upright in a glass dish. On both ends, she arranged young onions and radishes with their leaves still on them. She had filled in with peaches, apples, bananas, and grapes. Lastly she affixed a small sign to the top of the celery. The sign said on both sides, "No, no, don't touch. That is, until all else fails!"

Both girls stood back from the furniture and nodded their heads. Meg said, "It's good enough. Now to get our showers and dress before five o'clock. We just have twenty minutes."

Realizing how short their time was, they flew to their rooms to get started. Meg said she would shower first and then get out of Jean's way.

Chapter 5
The Party

There was a knock on the door before they were quite present-able. They neatened their rooms on the fly and rushed out to the porch where the earliest arrivals had sat down to wait.

"Why weren't you ready on time?" Bill asked.

Jean started explaining what had caused their lateness. She said, "Someone came last night after we were asleep and dumped out the plants, turned over the furniture and made a complete mess of this porch."

"It doesn't appear to have been in a mess. What really happened?" Gerald asked

Meg repeated much of what Jean had said, adding that they had been helped by a stranger who had just happened by. He was so helpful that he too, is invited to the party.

At just that moment, Nan and Mary Frances arrived and were greeted by all. Much hugging and kissing was going around.. Then the stranger arrived, causing a stir again.

Jesse was greeted and made at home. He seemed to fit right in with their other friends.

Jesse said in response, "I am already feeling right at home. Meg and Jean invited me on my good behavior. I hope I can live up to their expectations."

More and more folks were arriving. Jean lead the way indoors and invited all to help themselves to the refreshments. The punch bowl was still empty. Jean asked Jesse to help fill it. She showed him where the punch was and the ginger ale, too.

Soon everyone was served and finding seating in the living room and on the porch. Almost everyone had enjoyed dancing. The party lasted far past the expected hour. When someone noticed the late hour, everyone was of like mind. They all wanted to get back to their beds and get to sleep so they would be able to make it to classes tomorrow on opening day.

When all were gone, Jean and Meg began gathering things into trash cans. When they got to the kitchen to wash up the serving trays and put away all of the left overs, they found that Jesse was still there and was almost finished with the kitchen chores.

They were very thankful for his help. They thanked him profusely as they joined in to finish up. They chatted about the party and agreed that all had gone well. Jesse couldn't believe that all those refreshments had been prepared so quickly and done away with so quickly. He also had been impressed with all the guests. They had all seemed to be highly intelligent, a trait that Jesse perceived to be very important on a college campus.

Finally, all the guests were gone and they could now go to bed. That didn't take very long as they just undressed and jumped into bed in their pj's.

Chapter 6
First Class of the Year

Morning arrived far too early but they got up and dressed for their first day of classes which was to start in Shaw Hall at the other side of the campus, on the third floor reached only by flights of stairs.

Time was getting short when they arrived outside Dr. Bramlette's classroom. They entered quietly. The door was still open and all the seats were taken except for two. Someone motioned Meg toward her seat and Jean surmised that the other empty seat must be hers. Too, both girls were happy to see that Jesse was in their class.

Their instructor was seated at his desk. He rose and went to the windows, looked out and then turned to ask. "When did American History begin?"

No one answered him as they weren't sure just what he meant. Jesse raised his hand to gain permission to speak.

Dr. Bramlette spoke, "I don't believe I have met you but since we are all seated alphabetically, I know your name, Jesse Ray. Do you have an answer to my question?"

"Not exactly, sir. I want to know if you consider history to have begun when it was first written down."

Everyone else was just sitting and thinking. 'What did he mean by his question?' Jean was wondering if he meant, did history begin when the first white men arrived from Europe in 1492 or was it when the aborigines arrived earlier from Siberia when they crossed the straits into Alaska.

They were all surprised to hear their instructor say, "No, I meant, when did the history of the continent begin?"

Now some other students were raising their hands. Dr. Bramlette asked Gerald, "Do you know when the history of America began?"

Gerald answered, "I would have said in 1492, but since I didn't catch all of yours and Jesse's conversation, or was it when someone arrived who could record what was happening."

"That is very astute of you to answer my question with a question. Maybe we should look at the question again. When did American history begin?"

No one spoke. Everyone was searching their brains for the answer but were not anywhere close to arriving at the answer he wanted. At this rate class would end before he got an answer.

Meg finally raised her hand. Dr. Bramlette asked, "Meg, do you have an answer for us?

Meg had listened closely to everyone's contribution, including Dr. Bramlette. He had seemed to trigger her answer. "Yes, sir. Was it at the Creation of the world?"

Dr. Bramlette grinned from ear to ear. He said, "Young lady, you are exactly right. The story of our homeland and all the rest of the world began at Creation. Does anyone know just when that was?"

Jesse said, "Day one of year one."

"You, too, are correct. But when was that?" the instructor asked.

Jesse answered, "I don't know, but if you are in the habit of asking questions as far out as that one, I think I am in the wrong class."

Some of the class clapped their hands in agreement with Jesse. They too, had no idea as to the exact year that he meant. They just sat quietly awaiting their instructor's instruction about it.

Dr. Bramlette laughed loudly. When he could get his breath well enough to speak, he said, "I can see that we are going to have a grand old time this term in American History. History began so long ago that we now have astronomers, paleontologists, geolo-gist, and others who are working hard to find that answer. As far as I know right at this moment, they haven't got a clue as to the exact year the world was created. Some think it was at least 40,000 years ago. Others think the world is much older, maybe millions of years. However, that was a trick question, with a cause."

Chapter 7
Outside Reading Assignment

"I will be assigning outside reading assignments. I will be very specific about them. When the day comes to review what we have read, I will ask several questions based on the exact assignments. Only the persons who have read those particular portions will have the correct answer."

Jesse doubted that, but he didn't say anything right then.

Dr. Bramlette continued, "This has done more for my students than any series of lectures I could come up with. I am sure you will all be bound to do your assignment very carefully. I will give you the assignment on Wednesdays. You will be expected to have completed your studying by the following Wednesday. You will have completed it to the best of you ability so as to not miss the answer or have no answer at all."

Jesse wanted to pursue more information in order to fully understand just what they would be trying to do. He asked, "How many different assignments do you have to choose from?"

"Not as many as you might think, but enough to satisfy my cause. Did that answer your question?"

"No, sir. I was wondering how many assignments you make in each book?"

"Only the important ones." Dr. Bramlette answered. He added, "Are there anymore questions this morning before we begin?"

"Yes, sir. But I still do not understand how you arrive at your assignments, your questions, your answers and just how you know your answer is the correct one."

"Now that is just what I like to see in a history student. That is, delving into the innermost regions of my teaching. This way, all of you will read all of your assignments. I promise none of them will be very long, but I do make the question based on the most important part of that reading. This way we will be, killing two birds with one stone,' so to speak when you have found both the most important part for your question and its correct answer,. You will have to consider that as you read."

He continued, "I will explain just how I prepared for this portion of my instruction. First, I found all the books that where available in our library about all the areas of my history. I read all of them from cover to cover. As I read, I jotted down the pages that contained the question and its answer. I arranged with the librarian to have a specific location for all those books. I was very fortunate to get an alcove off the main library to shelve them. Some are Asian, European and World History as well as American History. The only students who are allowed in the alcove have to have a note in my handwriting with your name on it. They will be checking those notes regularly until they are familiar with all of you. This way you do not have to scurry around the entire library to locate your books. They are all in that room. You will return your book the same day that you go to get the next one. If you all do not do that, some of you will not find your book."

"Oh, yes. I was about to forget. Each one of you who answers my question correctly will get a 100, which will be treated the same as a test grade."

Then he went on to say, "I will have your new assignments on your desk each Wednesday. It will include exact pages to be read, and you will have a whole week to prepare. It will also include the Title and Author."

"Now, if you will open your textbooks to the preface, we will begin."

Everyone readily followed his directions. Then he said, "Read the Preface and write down a question based on what you feel is the most important part. Write your answer, also. Then close your books so I will know when all have finished."

He sat back in his seat as he observed all of us following his directions to the letter. When all the books were closed, he asked, "Bill, what is your question based on the most important part?"

Bill answered, "There was nothing there but generalities."

"You are exactly right. There was nothing but generalities there. Now, please turn to the first page of the first chapter. Read that page, write down your question based on the most important part. When finished, close your books again."

Dr. Bramlette noticed that Jean was the first to close her book. When all were finished and had their books closed, he asked Jean, "What was the most important part of that reading?"

Jean answered, "I would say that the most important part was the discovery of the land that was misnamed because the sailors thought that they were in India which is in Asia. They called the natives Indians, because of that belief and probably never found out for themselves that they were totally wrong."

"If you agree with Jean, raise your hands." Most of the class raised their hands.

"You are all wrong. A misinterpretation of such an occurrence is not factual. The answer should have been, 'After sighting land, the ship dropped anchor and the men came ashore.' Who can tell me why that is the correct answer?"

Bill raised his hand, "That is the only true facts given."

"You are exactly right.

Bill asked, "Is that a hint as to how we will be able to identify the most important fact in our reading assignments?"

Dr. Bramlette answered as he closed his book just as the closing bell rang. "Yes, it will put you on your toes to pinpoint just what is the most important information in your reading assignment, won't it?"

Chapter 8
Discombobulated

"My, how time flies when you are having fun!" Jesse remarked.

The rest of the class was busy copying their assignment based on their textbook from the board, that is, all except Jesse.

Their instructor said, "I believe all of you have the right idea. You are dismissed."

The class was silent as they left the building as all of them were trying to understand all that they had heard in class.

Meg declared, "I am discombobulated!"

All seemed to agree with her. They too, were discombobulated. The group continued up the brick walk silently.

Someone at the front of the group stopped and asked, "How are we to know how to do this correctly? Where do students congregate between classes? We need to ask some experienced former students how they managed those assignments."

It was Jesse. All the rest knew that answer. 'The Snack Shop'.

Jesse stepped aside to allow the students who knew the Snack Shop's whereabouts to lead the way.

When all were inside the Snack Shop, Jesse raised his voice loud enough to be heard above the babble of card players, visitors, and clerks who were filling orders.

When he could be heard, he asked, "Who among you have already taken Dr. Bramlette's American History class?"

Apparently almost all of them had experienced that. One guy asked, "He's up to no good again, is he?"

Several people made a remark or two. Some of the students who had been in the shop were facing the door through which we had entered, They were observing the arrival of Dr. Bramlette. A sort of hush fell on the group who knew he was there.

Dr. Bramlette asked, "Have you found out the answer to your questions?"

Jesse answered, "We haven't gotten to that yet. But how did you know where to find us?"

Dr. Bramlette was not deterred. He said, "I just wanted you to get the very best answer from the very best student present. Mary Ruth, would you be willing to answer this group's questions?"

Chapter 9
A Straight Answer

Mary Ruth answered, "I'll do my very best to do that."

"That's good enough for me." Dr. Bramlette said, "Go ahead. Ask away."

Everyone turned toward Jesse, since it was his idea. Jesse asked. "How do we go about preparing our do the outside reading assignments with accuracy on a regular basis?"

We were all awaiting Mary Ruth's answer. She cleared her throat a bit and hesitantly began to explain just how she had managed to do it. She explained, "First, you get the book from the library as soon as possible. You read the assignment several times the first day. You write down your question based on what you deem to be the most important fact. You write your answer. Later you read it again several times, each time you may change your mind about what is most important. Keep all of your questions and answers. Each day read it at least once and reconsider your idea. Reread your other questions so you can remember them all. When you get to class, if Dr. Bramlette asks about your fact, give him your answer. No one else will have the answer about what you have read. You will probably have the answer correct and receive your perfect score. At least, that is how I did it."

Dr. Bramlette said, "I have got to return to my classroom and write all that down before I forget it. I will use that for my lesson plan in the future."

As he left, the present class sighed in relief to have found some directions that made sense.

Chapter 10
An Unanswerable Question

All of the group was stirring about. Some were going on to their next class. Some were taking another players hand at bridge, as that player had to leave to get to the next class. Meg and Jean needed a cool drink. They had already placed their order when Jesse came over to get a soda. He insisted on paying for all of them. The girls warned him not to get in the habit of picking up their tab.

They had strolled outside to find a bench where they could all sit together while enjoying their sodas. They soon saw Dr, Bramlette almost running up the brick walk. Jesse asked if he had forgotten something.

"I surely did. Come along with me back to the shop." The three followed him. When they entered, there were a lot fewer people there than had been there earlier. He was breathing very hard but he began to speak anyway.

He said, "I believe that most of you are aware of a professor on campus who asks outlandish questions on his tests that have not been discussed in class." Someone said Dr. Seymour's name. He nodded and continued, "Yes. Now I have an assignment for all of my students in all of my history classes. You are the first to hear about it. I need to know how many salmon swim upstream to the place of their birth in any given year to spawn."

Some students didn't understand what he meant as they were not cognizant of the term 'spawn'. Some who did know its meaning, explained it. "That is when the mature fish come back from their two or three years in the sea, to breed, lay eggs, and leave the young to fend for themselves."

There ensued a lively sharing of information about salmon. The students listened well and then started deciding just how to go about finding the answer. Most went toward the library so Meg, Jesse and Jean went along, too.

There were folks looking at magazines, books, card catalogs and encyclopedias. Jesse just sat down alone at a table and started writing words on paper. Meg and Jean thought that was very odd. Meg asked, "Jean, what can he be doing?"

"I haven't got a clue. Let's ask him what he is doing."

They walked over to his table. He had several pages of note written down, but where was he getting his information? He didn't have any books except his history book.

Jean was curious about that. She asked, "Where did you get all that information"

"Out of my head." Jesse answered.

"What are you writing about?" Meg wanted to know.

"About salmon and their habits." Jesse answered

"Do you mean that you already know all that information about salmon?"

"Well, yes. I have read a lot about salmon over the years. I wanted to review what I already knew before starting to find Doc's answer."

"What did you find out?"

"I found that I had read almost nothing about spawning."

Meg and Jean drifted away from Jesse in order to find a reference book on spawning. While looking, Bill came over to see if he could help them in any way.

Chapter 11
Perhaps It Can Be Solved

Bill and Jean had dated some last year. Jean liked him a lot but she wasn't one to call much attention to herself. Meg had gone back to Jesse's side, so Jean and Bill were alone among the stacks of books. Bill hadn't located anything and wanted to know how Jean was progressing.

Jean was glad that they were in history class together. She wondered if their paths would cross in any of their other classes. She explained, "I have found no help here in this library. Have you found anything?"

Bill was shaking his head. Then he said, "I really do not think we'll find his answer here, do you?"

"One thing is for sure. I don't believe he found his question here either."

"Where else should we look?" Bill asked.

"I have no clue." Jean said. Then she remembered that she had a class in gym next period. "But Meg and I have to go to the gym soon."

Bill joined Jean as she walked over to Jesse's table to remind Meg about gym class. Meg and Jesse didn't see them coming as they were engrossed in his notes. When they looked up and saw Jean with Bill, Jesse asked, "What have we here?"

Bill responded, "You surely don't think you have the corner on the market for beautiful girls, do you?"

"No, no. I am just glad that you don't either." The guys were just joshing, they were really pretty good friends to have not known each other but a few hours.

Jean asked, "Meg, are you about ready for gym? And remember we have to go shopping again today to restock our larder."

"Okay, let's get to it." With that they waved goodby to the guys and rushed off but they really would have liked to stick around with Jesse and Bill.

Bill asked, "Jesse, do you think we have that fishy answer here in this library?"

"No. These notes are things about salmon that I have learned over the years. It's not here either."

Bill suggested, "Maybe, Dr. Bramlette has seen something about salmon on TV recently."

Jesse jumped to his feet, whacked Bill on his arm and said, "That's it. After I arrived back home from Iraq, I watched a documentary on the University channel. It was all about spawning. I don't know how I failed to think of that film. I'll bet Blockbuster has it in stock. I'll call and ask them about it."

Bill walked with him toward the pay phone. He said, "If it's there, I'll drive you over to get it."

After Jesse's call had received an affirmative answer, they both almost ran to Bill's car. They visited about the girls, about salmon, about 'When did American History Begin?" and found they had a lot in common. Bill had grown up on a farm also. They both were interested in those two girls from Murphy.

After returning to campus, they both walked down to Jean's and Meg's house to see if they had finished their shopping. When they arrived, there was no one at home. They sat on the porch and rocked.

Soon the shoppers returned. Both men assisted with their burdens and then Jesse had an announcement to make. "Bill and I have some news to share. We think we have found a source that will answer Doc's question."

Chapter 12
Getting Ready for Another Party

The girls squealed loudly before saying, "How did you find it?"

Bill said he had helped a little but he asked Jesse to tell them all about their find.

"You know, I had written a lot of notes from memory, but I failed to remember the most recent salmon information I had learned. After I returned home from Iraq, we were watching the University channel. They showed a documentary about salmon and spawning. I called Blockbuster to see if they had it in stock. They did and Bill offered to drive me to town to get it. Here it is."

"How do we want to get the information to the whole class?" Jean asked.

They all had some ideas that they willingly shared, After a time, Jesse asked, "Could we invite the class to watch it with us?"

"Oh, that is a good idea." Meg said. "When should we do it?"

Jean suggested, "How about tonight about seven? We could drag out some refreshments and maybe fix some more, too. If we get a message to all the dorm offices and ask them to announce on their sound systems that our history class is invited here to see a film about salmon, and ask the dorm students to ask their friends who do not live in dorms, to join us, too. What do you think?"

Jesse asked, "Isn't that pushing it a bit? But I don't really know of a better time and place."

All agreed and wanted to know what needed to be done before the crowd arrived?

The girls already had their paper to jot down just what needed to be prepared on such short notice. Everyone made suggestions. The resulting plan included: cook some more food, get the serving tables ready, get the film set up, get a bite of supper, and then they would be ready for anything.

Jesse offered to prepare supper if they had a suggestion as to the menu. Jean said, "Would bacon, eggs, and toast with jelly be adequate for supper?"

All agreed and all went to the kitchen to get the jobs done.

Meg got the groceries out for Jesse and the pans, utensils, etc. She and Jean were discussing what they would need to do to get the party food ready. It was decided that they would work on the back porch while Jesse cooked. They could get the left over foods ready and then they could make some brownies. Bill offered to run to the grocery store to pick up soft drinks, and anything else they would need.

Meg suggested that he get an assortment of cookies and thirty apples so everyone would have that to nibble on, too

Everyone got busy with their assignment and soon supper was ready, the groceries were delivered,, the veggies and fruit trays were arranged and everyone was glad to get a plate of Jesse's goodies, a canned drink, and go to the back porch to eat under the shade trees together.

It was fun having both Bill and Jesse with them and all working together to get ready for the movie hour. They were really ready for their guests before the first arrivals.

Chapter 13
The Film, the Food, the Facts

The dorm students had gotten both messages and acted on them. Almost everyone was present. When all were inside and seated on furniture or on the floor, Jesse started to tell them something about the film. He said they would be seeing wonderful scenery, a lot of fish, some dams that would be a problem for the fish to overcome, and to remember the question, "How many salmon return to their place of birth to spawn?"

He promised that after the film, they would all discuss it and come to a consensus of opinion for to the answer.

Everyone seemed satisfied with all that, so he flipped the switch and the show began. It was about an hour long. After the show everyone was invited to get a plate of food and a drink to work on while they discussed it. That really went well. Soon all had returned to the living room to eat and talk about the show.

Jesse said, "I've had a busy day. I'll finish my plate before beginning the discussion." The sounds were all happy and excited about really being able to find the answer in the film.

There were some small group discussions during the meal. When Jesse had finished, he stood near the television to begin their discussion.

He imitated Dr. Bramlette as he asked, "How many salmon returned to the place of their birth to spawn?"

The group imitated themselves as they had reacted to Dr, Bramlette's question. No one said anything.

That brought on a chuckle and another question from Jesse. He asked, "Does anyone have an idea to share with the whole group?"

Bill bravely spoke up, saying, "I think Doc must have seen this film or one very much like it to find that question. No one can possibly know the exact number of fish but with some thought as to all of the problems that the fish faced we should be able to come up with a percentage of the fish that made the entire journey."

"Well put, Bill. Did all of you like the scenery?" Lots of agreement was exhibited by nodding heads.

"What problems were caused by the man-made dams?" Several girls spoke to that but mostly with questions about why there had to be dams that caused such big problems. There were questions about the fish ladders (step like shelves with water in them in order for the fish to continue upstream and get past the dams that the ladders were attached to) that helped the fish climb over the dams very gradually. There were questions about how you could tell a male fish from a female fish. That brought on the discussion of the toothsome fighters who were adamantly proving that they had the upper fin.

Everyone really wanted to have that answer down pat before going back to their dorms. Some people were raising their hands in order to be heard. Jesse didn't know all their names but he did know a lot of them. Everyone got to say what they had on their mind. After about 45 minutes, Jesse began trying to summarize the thoughts of the group.

"Do you all agree that the food supply was a very important part of the entire trip? One, because it was many miles of travel. Two, the same food sources were not available all along the way. Three, they tended to interfere with each other over food."

"What part did the various kinds of water play in the trip?" Gerald named the differences. He said. "The mature salmon were swimming in the salty sea where they had lived for two or three years. There are currents in the sea that alter the way the fish could swim. But those rushing rivers, with rapids and water falls were exhausting for the fish. The shallow, slow moving streams had a happy effect. All the fish seemed to swim better there. The man made waterways were effective for them as there would not have been any hope for them to get beyond the dams without the fish ladders."

"If all of the fish had gotten to their destination, that would have been 100% of the fish. Who would give us your best guess as to what percent you think made the trip all the way?", Jesse asked.

Meg said, "I think a large percentage of them got to the quiet lake. I'd guess right around 90% made it all the way."

"What do you use to figure that percentage?" Jesse asked.

"I considered their food supply, the distance to swim, the various waterways, and the problems caused by the male fish's bites." someone in the back of the room answered.

"Does anyone have any changes to make in that answer?"

A hush fell over the group. Someone asked Meg to restate her answer.

Meg said it again. "I think a large percentage of them got to the quiet lake. I would guess around 90% made it all the way."

Chapter 14
Recitation

Jesse asked again if that was what we wanted to tell Dr. Bramlette in the morning.

Bill suggested, "I think we should say Meg's answer and also the problems that they had to overcome, too."

Jesse said, "Okay! We think a large percentage of them got to the quiet lake. About 90% overcame the food supply problems, the traveling conditions, and the biting fish in order to arrive in the waters of the quiet lake."

Almost everyone stood and cheered our successful conclusion. Everyone was writing it down in order to memorize it so they'd be able to recite it with the rest tomorrow morning in history class.

Everyone was thanking Meg and Jean for their hospitality and good food and Jesse for remembering the film. They gradually took their leave. Meg and Jean were thinking that tomorrow would be here before we're ready for it we don't get our rest.

Jesse was the last one to depart. He said his thanks and said good night.

There had been lots of help clearing up things after we had eaten. The trash was all in the proper place, the left overs were refrigerated, and the serving dishes were waiting to be washed after classes tomorrow when Jesse could be there to help.

The tired Meg and Jean got to bed and to sleep in record time. But, oh how early their clocks alarmed!!! Up they got and off did trot to History Class to recite their answer with all the rest.

The whole class arrived and waited impatiently for Dr. Bramlette. When he did arrive, which was really on time, he was surprised to find so many early students. He started off by saying, "I had promised you folks that I would have your first outside reading assignments on your desks when you arrived on Wednesday. I still have them."

Bill asked, "Would it be alright if we pass them around? That is, if they are arranged alphabetically."

Gerald suggested, "Let's try that. It just may help you out every week if we can do it correctly."

When all were seated, Dr. Bramlette gave the neatly stacked cards to Alma Atkins. Soon they were all distributed and all seemed to have the one with their name on it.

"It's a pity that I hadn't tried that long ago. You folk got it done much faster than I do when I have to walk across each row and place the cards neatly on the desks. I say a big thank you to all of you."

That is when it happened. Dr. Bramlette sat at his desk and asked, "How many salmon returned to their place of birth to spawn?"

We all got to our feet and said in unison, "About 90% overcame the problems of food supply, traveling problems, and biting fish to arrive in the quiet lakes of their birth."

The class sat back down. Nobody spoke. Dr. Bramlette just sat staring straight ahead.

Then he arose, cleared his throat, and asked, "How did you all know that answer which is certainly the correct answer?"

Bill answered, "We owe our thanks to Jesse Ray. He remembered a documentary on your subject."

Chapter 15
The First Outside Reading Assignment Completed

"And just how did you do that, Jesse Ray?" Dr. Bramlette asked.

Jesse answered, "I am gifted with having a photographic memory. When we got to the library to seek our answer, I wrote down all the facts about salmon that I have read or been told of all my life. I didn't have the spawning answer. When Bill suggested that you may have seen a movie about it, it jogged my memory. I had seen a documentary on the University channel after returning from Iraq."

Dr. Bramlette sat up straight and asked, "I have never had a student with a photographic memory. I have noticed that you do not bother to take notes, record assignments, or fail to know all the answers to my questions. But I had not arrived at the reason for that. Now I know. What else can your gift do for you?"

Jesse answered, "That would be too much to explain during class. Maybe we could discuss it in private, later."

"Yes. That would be a good idea. I have taught for more than forty years and have never had one such as you."

Then Dr, Bramlette led a discussion about the film and everyone took part. That was a lively class. He seemed thrilled that we had found the film in order to find the answer together. He did caution us that that method would not be acceptable for our outside reading assignments.

That led the way for a discussion concerning that first assignment which we had received today. He told us, using Mary Ruth's words, just what we should do to be sure to have the correct question and answer every time.

After the bell sounded, everyone quietly gathered their books and left. Meg said as we arrived on solid ground, " Today, I am not discombobulated."

We nodded our heads in agreement and hurried on past the Snack Shop toward the library. On arrival at the Alcove, we found that the books were easy to locate and we were all soon seated around some of the tables to commence following Mary Ruth's directions.

On comparing our textbooks to our reference books out of the Alcove, we decided that these library books were pretty far advanced by comparison. The authors adeptly related the knowledge they had attained in a manner that proved helpful to the well read and well educated group. But of course, that remained to be seen.

All of us had met with all our classes at least once by this time. Meg and Jean both had copies of Bill's and Jesse's schedules so they would know what everyone was doing at any given time. Of course, Jesse hadn't needed to record the schedules since he was so gifted.

Meg and Jean just had to know more about 'photographic memory'. They brought up that subject. Jesse decided it would be best to humor them and describe that phenomenon. Before attacking the subject that all were so curious about, he suggested that they go find a comfy place to sit outside to hear all about it.

He really wanted to discuss it with just Meg, Jean and Bill, but a lot of the classmates also wanted to hear about it. Jesse asked them to lead the way to find a fitting arena for his discussion of the topic at hand.

Someone suggested the amphitheater. We rushed down to that area of the campus. Jesse had not seen it before. He was impressed. Meg and Jean had taken part in two productions there and were quite used to its charm.

When all were seated in the shade in the the elevated rows of seats, Jesse asked if anyone had particular questions about his memory problem. No one, not even Jesse looked upon it as a problem. Several questions were asked, Jesse answered loudly enough for all to hear. The first question had to do with how he had gotten that gift. Jesse just said, "I was born with it. You either have it or you don't. It seems that one person in each generation in my family, gets the gift. The gene that carries it came to America with the Pilgrims. The cabin boy on the Mayflower had it. Henry Samson married and one of his children got it, too. My Grandmother Armstrong was born a Samson about two hundred and twenty years later and was 'so gifted'.

He explained, "No record was kept as to which person in every generation has been so gifted, but by word of mouth it was handed down. My Mother, Margaret Armstrong Ray, told us what she had learned about it over the years and was so happy that she had a son who was 'so gifted'. That also meant that our family would be passing it on to future generations. I am the only one who inherited that gene in my generation. So only my children will carry it on."

There were other questions to follow. One was, "How does it help you in your daily life?"

Jesse said, "I do not have to take notes. I do not have to refer to schedules to keep up with my daily schedule. I do not have to jot down phone numbers to be able to get in touch with friends. I don't need a list when I shop. I can remember directions once I have learned them as to how to get from here to anywhere. It saves lots of time so that I can do other things while the rest of you are doing those sorts of things."

"While I was serving in the army, my commanding officer questioned me often on how I knew what he had said to me three or four days ago. I explained that I had been born with this gift. He didn't have any reference books to rely on to find out all about photographic memory. So we had a session somewhat like this one. He questioned and I answered.. Do we have any more questions?"

"Oh, yes." Meg was speaking. "How can we learn how to do it?"

"You can not learn it. You either have it or you don't."

Jean asked, "Why is it called photographic memory? You also seem to have a phonographic memory. Just how does that work?"

"The eyes and the ears are pretty closely associated. The same part of my brain does both things. If I see or hear anything, I remember it for always"

He continued, "That sounds like all that would be happy stuff. Not so!! All of the bad things I have been subjected to, are still instilled in my head. I often have flashbacks about the deaths of my fellow soldiers, members of our family who have been ill and died , and troublesome things that are unsolvable."

"It sort of sounds like it gives me some godlike powers. It doesn't. You probably have sought answers to your questions. You have fallen short of the mark in finding what would solve your problem. It just never leaves me alone. I have to really work at those sorts of things to get them out of my head and make room for normal thoughts.

All in all, I suppose it is more of a blessing than a handicap. At least, it does help me not to have to delve into my studies as diligently as more normal human beings. Now are there further questions?"

Some folk began remarking about what Jesse had said and telling how they had felt about it. They were about to decide that they were blessed with not having a photographic memory when it became problematic.

Jesse said, "Now you're talking!! Its not like all the rest of humanity falls short of the grace of God, for not being like me."

Chapter 16
Love is in the Air

Our group had dwindled away during the discussion as people had had to go to other classes. We, who were left, decided to go to the snack shop for a soda and then get on with our day.

Jean asked Meg, "What do we have next?"

Meg answered, "Nothing except getting some much needed rest and getting started with our outside reading assignments."

That statement reminded all of us that we had things to do and places to go. The group left with the happy thought that we would be together every Monday, Wednesday, and Friday in American History, and that one week may not be long enough with all our other subjects, to get the correct question and answer from our outside reading. Yet everyone was set to get started with it and not put it off any longer.

Since Meg and Jean were following the same course of study in the same major, all of their classes were the same. It was just Tuesday and another 24 hours before another history class. The girls agreed that that was proving to be problematic in spite of the fact that they needed to get started on their outside reading assignment and their assignments for their other classes. They were both glad that they didn't have another party tonight.

Their classes were finally completed for today. They went to the library to study. Jesse was there. He had some reference work to do for another of his classes.

When he saw them enter the library, he came over to invite them to join him at his table. Meg asked, "You are sure that we won't get in your way?"

"Best friends never get in the way. What are you two looking for?" was Jesse's welcoming answer.

Jean answered, "I'll get our books and be right back." She left Jesse and Meg while she went to get the two books to use for their assignments.

When she started back with her books, she met Bill. Bill and Jean had dated for a while last spring. Bill had noticed that both Meg and Jesse were seemingly engrossed in each other, so he invited Jean to join him at his table for a few minutes.

Jean was a bit surprised, but pleased, also. They sat at a table near the windows a little distance from Meg and Jesse.

Bill asked, "How are things going?"

"We have enjoyed our other classes. We know some of the students but this is a new bunch of professors."

Bill agreed that that was sort of where he was coming from, too. Then he said, "That's the way life is. Some good and some bad."

Jean was surprised to hear his answer. She asked, "Why do you feel that way?"

"You already know, don't you?"

"Know what?" Jean asked.

"How much I like you! When I saw both of you girls so engrossed with Jesse, I figured I was 'hung out to dry."

"Oh, what a strange way you have of telling me what you are thinking."

"I thought that Jesse was cutting in on my girl! Wasn't he?"

Jean was trying to figure out where he was coming from. She asked, "Do you mean that you thought that I was interested in Jesse the same way Meg is?"

"Yes, but I want you to be my girlfriend. I want that to become an established fact."

"I am honored, sir. I would like to be your steady."

Bill glanced around to see who was looking before he took Jean into his arms. They embraced momentarily. Jean was a little shaken up. She usually understood how people perceived her. Why had she not noticed? And at this rate they would never get their assignments completed.

She asked, "Would it be better for us to get farther apart so that we can get our minds on the work at hand?"

"Oh, no, don't you see that Jesse and Meg are hard at work with their books?"

"But I have Meg's book. What could she be doing?"

They both decided to go to see if Meg needed her book or not. When they arrived at their table, they found both Meg and Jesse doing crossword puzzles.

Jean asked, "Is that what you two came here to do?"

Jesse looked up and said, "No, but Meg had nothing better to do while she awaited your bringing her book. What took so long?"

Then with a questioning look, he asked, "Is there something you wanted to tell us?"

"Yes, Bill and I have decided to resume our dating this year."

"What brought that on?" Meg asked.

Jean and Bill just walked away after glancing briefly at each other.

Chapter 17
Double Date

A short time later, Meg and Jesse came over to their table to join them. Jesse suggested. "We are trying to get through this day and on to tomorrow. Is that what you are doing?"

Meg added, "We decided that time flies when you are having fun. Would you two like to join us on a hike to view the river and the island at the river bend?

We soon found our way across the small hill that separated the main campus from the river.

"I had not been made aware that there was such a place near here. When Meg told me about it, we both thought it might be fun to go to investigate. What do you think?" Jesse remarked.

Jesse was somewhat impressed with the scenery. Fall was not too far off. Some leaves were trying to change color. We tarried until hunger reminded us that the day was getting on and that we should all get back to the business at hand.

Bill suggested, "Let's get my car and all go into town for lunch."

We all thought that that would be a welcome change. We retraced our steps back to campus, got into Bill's car and went to a favorite restaurant in town where lots of students liked to hang out.

We all enjoyed our meal which none of us had had to cook. When we returned to campus, we all decided to go to our college homes and get ready for tomorrow.

Chapter 18
A Lecture, Voice Lesson, and a Drama Class

The next time for history class came quite early . We were to have read the entire first chapter. We had done that and were pleasantly surprised when Dr. Bramlette lectured the entire period on that chapter and included lots of information to support his talk.

Our discussion on the way up the hill that day had to do with wondering if he, too, had a photographic memory. And too, he had announced a test for Friday on Chapter 1.

We scattered to go to our college homes or to another class. Meg and Jean didn't have a class until after lunch, so they just went home.

They decided to do their reading. That all went well except for their worrying about just what was the most important idea in that reading. Still following Mary Ruth's advice, they jotted a question down and its answer. Later they would repeat all that many times before next Wednesday.

They were really eager to get to their next class. It was a voice lesson. They were remembering that they had neither had time to sing at all since they got back on campus. That prompted them to sing Ave Maria together. They had no accompaniment, but they completed the whole thing and were pleased to find they had not lost their voices.

At the auditorium where their voice and acting classes met, they were happy to see some students from last year there. They had not seen most of them since returning to school.

They had fun visiting with them and also with their voice lessons. They were pleased when their instructors found them to be in good voice after a summer at home.

Later they would meet with their acting class and hopefully find out about the next production they would be involved in. They had done some really delightful plays during their first two years and had been promised that the next ones would be even more fun. They couldn't ever imagine what the instructor had had in mind.

This was their only class with a lady instructor. She really seemed to know her stuff when directing a play. They really hadn't thought about how this year in acting would be.

When class started, they soon found out that they would do two productions a semester. That sounded like a lot. How were they to continue their dating and partying with all of this hard work?

Meg and Jean remained after class in hopes that they might speak with Professor James. While they waited, they decided to ask her some questions about her planned productions. They knew that they were a required part of the course. In fact they were the major part. Last year they had had no social conflicts to stand in their way.

Jean suggested to Meg, "Maybe we could alter our schedule by dropping this course or postponing it until later."

Meg wanted to know, "How would that help us? It is a required course and our future courses depend on it"

Jean said, "I guess that I forgot all about that. I suppose we will just have to go ahead as is."

At just that moment, Professor James had sent her assistant to bring the girls into her office. They went but what were they to say?

As they were shone into her office, she asked, "Do you girls have some sort of magical powers that have brought you here to day?"

Both girls just shook their heads negatively. Meg asked, "Why do you ask that?"

"I have just completed my plans for our first production, 'The Sound of Music,' I want both of you to take the starring roles and use your marvelous voices to sing duets. What do you think about that?"

They were both speechless. They had never even thought they would get the leading role until maybe next year. Jean asked, "Do you really mean it?"

"Of course I do. You two were the best of the best in our spring production last year. I most can't wait to see how it all comes together." She looked at a note on her desk, and asked, "Why did you wish to see me today?"

Meg said, "We are both dating this year and we are wondering if that would alter our activity here. But we will find some really good way to work around that."

Mrs. James smiled sweetly and said, "I am happy for you. You do want to do this play in the starring positions, don't you?"

"Yes ma'am. We will put all of our best effort into it. Thank you for making us your star players." With that, they stood up, and Meg asked if they might be excused.

Mrs. James came around her desk to bid them goodbye for now.

The girls left rather slowly but happily. They just couldn't wait to tell Bill and Jesse.

Chapter 19
How to Tell Their Good News

They hurried to find them but they weren't in the library. They got out the boy's schedules to check where they might be. They both had math classes this period. That sort of upset them but maybe it would be better for them to calm down and plan just how to go about telling them their good news.

As they walked along toward home, they discussed having dinner for the guys to night. Meg said, "We haven't got much to go on in the refrigerator so what are you thinking about for the menu?"

Jean suggested, "One of us could go to the store while the other cleans up and sets the table. I could shop if you will help me decide what to buy."

"We could do that barbecued chicken that we did for our parents this past summer. What do you think, Meg?"

Meg remembered what a hit that menu turned out to be. Too, it was a quick meal to prepare. "I say let's go for it."

They started writing their list before they came in sight of their house. The ingredients were partially already in the house. They just needed potatoes, cabbage chicken, and maybe some rolls to really get the guys attention.

On arriving at home, they saw no one on the deck. They knew the guys were still in their last class. Jean checked the refrigerator and cabinets to be sure that they needed only vegetables, buns and the chicken.

Jean told Meg, "I'm off to the store, now. I'll be back before you know it."

Meg started working on the items that were at hand. By the time Jean returned, she had dessert in the oven and a centerpiece partially finished made of late blooming weeds that grew everywhere. Queen Anne's lace is really too pretty to be considered a weed. Too, arranged with some branches of the shrubs that grew around their house, it had turned out quite well.

They discussed whether it would be necessary to get in touch with the fellows or just wait and see if they arrived unheralded.

They didn't have long to wait. Bill and Jesse were at the door. When they knew there was to be a good supper, they asked what they could do to help.

Jean pointed out that just visiting would be enough to keep them busy. There were no seats in the kitchen so they all went into the living room except Jean who was still busy with the slaw. The chicken had to cook a bit longer, so she joined the rest in the living room. They still had to tell them about their starring roles in one of this semester's productions. Instead, they asked Bill and Jesse if their classes were exciting in any way.

Jesse answered for both of them, "No way. What could possibly make math exciting?"

Bill said, "Having Jean and Meg in those classes."

"Well put, but that is impossible as they have other plans." Jesse mused.

The girls glanced toward each other and spoke simultaneously, "Our drama class will be exciting for us. We are to star in the leading roles and also sing duets."

"When will that be?"

"As yet unknown, but we will reserve you two, two of the best seats in the house.

Bill, how was your seat last year?"

Bill had to think a bit before saying, "I could see all of the show and I liked two of the actresses, but it would have been better to have had Jean beside me watching instead of on stage."

Jean was tense when she asked, "You knew I was in that class and would have to perform. You also told me you thought I did a good job. Wasn't that good enough?"

"I knew I was having 'foot in mouth disease' before I said that. Jesse and I will get used to all your practicing and performing, but we don't necessarily have to like it, do we?" Bill cringed a little as he had spoken.

Jesse asked, "You can't be involved in the practicing and productions if you are not taking that class, can you?"

Meg explained, "We do have non-class members as stage hands, photographers, and for some other stuff. Would you like to be involved?"

"Of course we would if we could be there when needed and not be interfering with our schedules," Jesse said.

"I never knew that last year. Did it just start this year?" Bill asked.

Jean was trying to get if they were serious or just teasing. She asked, "Are you two serious about being involved?"

Both Jesse and Bill said, "Dead serious!"

Meg spoke up to ask, "Do you two want us to sign you up for two of the positions? I understand they are not paid positions."

"We'll look into it ourselves if you have no objection," answered Bill.

That, settled for now, the girls went to the kitchen to check on their dinner. It was time to eat and the food was all ready. They said, "Come and get it."

After enjoying the good food and the good company, everyone took things to the kitchen. With all four helping, the kitchen was a bit crowded, but a good crowded. Soon all was back to normal, food put away, dishes done and they were ready to relax.

Bill went out on the deck. He came right back in with a hand full of movies from Blockbuster. After showing them his offerings, it was decided that they should all settle back and enjoy one of them.

Chapter 20
Discussing Outside Reading Assignments

After viewing 'An American in Paris', they decided to talk a bit about their outside reading assignments.

Jesse wanted to go first. He began by telling them about his entire reading from memory, Then he stated his question and its answer. That took all of about five minutes. Then he continued on other topics. He stated the questions and the answers. It was really interesting, but the other three seemed disturbed by it some way.

Jesse asked, "What have I done wrong?"

The others all asked, "How did you get ours, too?

"Is that what I did?" He asked sort of sheepishly.

"You know you did but we do not know when you could have read our books. When did you?"

Jesse hung his head and said, "While we were studying in the library. Jean you and Meg had left your books on my table. It was a bit more difficult to get Bill's book but he didn't notice that I picked it up during math class, I just did it to save you all some time. Is that bad?"

"Yes, it's bad. We want to share and share alike, but our memory won't let us do it your way. Of course, we won't have to question our question this time, you have already told us what it is."

"I won't do it again, if you would rather I didn't." Jesse offered.

Meg said, "It might come in handy when we are really involved in plays and singing. We might even ask you to do it for us then."

Bill was still trying to figure it out. He asked, "Do you mean that that bunch of assignments were that easy for you? I have already read mine three times and haven't yet found out what the question should be. Now I guess that I already know."

Jesse finally conceded that he knew it would be more meaningful for each one to do our own assignments. He added, "I'll help any time I'm needed."

That settled, they all became quiet and worked on other assignments. Meg and Jean read their assignment and decided Jesse had 'hit the nail on the head' with his rendition. They just wrote it down and were ready to answer just in case Dr. Bramlette asked their question.

The guys left about 10:00 PM to return to their rooms. The girls finished their day by just falling into bed. They did change into pj's first.

Chapter 21
The First History Test

Life returned to some semblance of normalcy until Friday when they would have their first test on United States History at 8 AM. The whole class seemed keyed up as they awaited their test on Chapter 1. Dr. Bramlette was in good form. He greeted the class with a sheaf of papers in his hand. They were his history tests. He made a couple of announcements. One had to do with another of his history classes who had tried to find the same answer we had found about salmon and spawning. They had reported to him that there were no references in the library that spoke to his question. He said that he had informed them that one other class had had better results but he did not tell them our answer or where we had found the answer.

Dr. Bramlette waved his fist full of papers in the air and asked, "Are you ready?"

"Yes, let's get on with our first test." Jesse suggested.

Dr. Bramlette answered, "Oh, you. Do you already have all the answers?"

"We won't know until you grade the papers, now will we?" The rest of us wanted to have as much time as possible to work on the test. We all clapped our hands in agreement with Jesse.

"Okay. Good luck to each of you." He handed several tests to the persons at the end of each row of seats and then went to his desk to rest while we figured out our answers.

Meg took one look at her test and felt like screaming. There were only ten questions. She would have to get 8 or 9 right, for sure. She read through them quickly, decided that she might make a 100. and started to work. The rest of the class followed suit. Soon the only sounds were pencils writing rapidly on paper. No one stopped working on the test until the bell rang, not even Jesse. Dr. Bramlette went to the door to receive the test papers.

Some students just smiled at him as they turned over their papers, some students said well wishes for a good weekend, some students sympathized with him for having to grade papers all weekend.

No matter the salutations to Doc, all of us were glad that that was over and had the feeling that our grades would be pretty good.

Jesse was the first to speak as we descended the stairs, "That went well, don't you think?"

Someone behind us said, "You are a good one to talk. You probably aced the whole thing."

"I really feel that all of us have a good chance at a perfect score. The test was the outline for his lecture, don't you think?" Jesse responded.

All the rest of us stopped walking and looked at each other. Jean asked, "Did any of you notice that before Jesse mentioned it?"

Bill said, "No, but by golly, I do believe he is right. That photographic memory does have to keep cropping up, doesn't it?"

Others said a few words and then grew quiet in order to let someone else be heard.

Someone suggested that we ask Jesse to hear our answers to see if he approves of them. We glanced about and found that Jesse had arrived at the Snack Shop already. Amber asked, "Could we ask him to go with us to the amphitheater again where all of us could participate equally?"

Lots of heads nodded in agreement and our feet got to moving again in the direction Jesse had gone.

We had stuck together and were all of like mind, it seemed. When we were all inside the Snack Shop, Bill went over to Jesse to ask him our question. He agreed with Bill and waved all of us to follow them.

Meg caught up with Jean and asked, "Do you feel like we are re'enacting the 'Pied Piper of Hamlin'?

Chapter 22
Discussing the Test

Those close by, agreed with Meg but we all kept moving toward 'Hamlin' anyway. When we had all arrived at the amphitheater, Jesse and Bill had been making a plan for all of us to follow.

Bill announced, "Jesse has agreed to ask one question from the test at a time and then all who wish may give their answer. If we get them right, he'll ask another of the questions, and so forth. If he can state a better answer, he will. Okay?"

We had all taken a seat and applauded Bill's announcement. Jesse stood and asked the first question. "Describe the voyage of the Nina, the Pinta, and the Santa Maria."

Lots of students were willing to describe what they could of the voyage. Jesse listened and then said, "I believe a concise statement formed of your combined statements would be, 'The wooden sailing ships, the Nina, the Pinto, and the Santa Maria, had been obtained by the Spanish King and Queen from Granada, a town they had defeated in the war. The Santa Maria was the lead ship. By the time Columbus had sailed as far as the Canary Islands, the Nina had to have a new rudder and the Pinta needed some square rigging. They had planned to stop at that port to get provisions but had a longer stay to remedy the ships' problems. Their diet was meager, their fears were great, as they feared that they would fall off the edge of the sea into an abyss. When Columbus sited a light which he believed was a campfire on dry land, the sailors were joyous to soon set foot on dry land after 33 days at sea."

There followed some discussion about his answer. When all grew quiet, Jesse asked the second question. "What were the items the crew found of interest on that island?"

Again there were many suggestions made. Jesse made a concise answer from all of the answers. He said, "There were food items that the men were not knowledgeable of. For example, animals and plants they had never seen, brightly colored parrots, ornaments made by the people, and gold."

The third question was, "What were the major problems they faced on shore?"

The group shared their suggestions and then Jesse said, "Their major problems were their inability to understand the languages. One of the ships ran aground and had to be destroyed. A fort was built of its timbers to house the crew of 39 sailors who remained in the new world when the others returned to Spain."

Question four was, "For what did the crew make an apology to Christopher Columbus?"

Jesse accepted Gerald's answer, "The crew apologized for mistrusting Columbus and for their great fear of the unknown and seemingly endless sea."

Question five was, "What new problems appeared on the trip back to Portugal?"

Bill said, "Both the Nina and the Pinta were damaged in the stormy passage and arrived back in Portugal at two different harbor towns. They later met again and proceeded to visit with the Spanish Royal Family'." Jesse seemed to accept his answer and went on to the next.

Question six was, ""What gifts did Columbus and his crews bring back from the New World?

This time Meg had the correct answer. She said, "They took gold, brightly colored feathers, parrots, strange plants and animals, Indian cloth, handcrafted Indian ornaments and a few Indians."

Question ten was, "What happened when Columbus attempted to again sail to Asia?"

Several people gave their answers but were told by Jesse that they were incorrect. Jesse said, "Columbus sailed west across the Gulf of Mexico and lost two ships off the Coast of what is now known as Central America. His two remaining ships tried to return eastward toward Jamaica but their poor condition caused them to run aground and were lost. Columbus was returned to Spain on someone else's ship. The Royal House of Spain no longer honored him. He had obtained a lot of gold and lived comfortably until his death in1506.'"

We all had gained much from that question and answer session. We thanked Jesse for helping us. We all figured he had aced the test and that most of us had not. We anxiously awaited the return of our tests on Monday.

Chapter 23
Partially Right

That was an exceedingly long weekend, but we were all 'bright eyed and bushy tailed ' when we arrived at Shaw Hall before 8 o'clock Monday morning. We were pleasantly surprised to find Dr. Bramlette had arrived ahead of us and was ready to return our tests. He said very little until after we all had looked at our papers While he sat at his desk watching our reactions, he had a strange look on his face. When he finally spoke, He said, "I was glad to see that seven of you made perfect scores. Would you seven be kind enough to stand.?"

No one seemed to move for a bit. Jesse looked around to see where the other six folks were. When he stood at last, the rest took to their feet. They were all on the back row, except Jesse. Dr. Bramlette asked those six people to remain after class for a conference with him. The rest of us were glad we had not made perfect scores.

During class, we were introduced to the second chapter of our book. Some of the class seemed to have found some time to read it ahead of class time. Meg and Jean wondered when they had found the time. Of course, Jesse was no surprise to them to be among that group. Dr, Bramlette showed us a filmstrip based on the architecture of early America. It showed several kinds of Indian dwellings, as well as the early cabins and fortresses of the white settlers. Class moved along faster than ever. We were anxious to compare our tests with Jesse's test. We went to the snack shop to get a beverage and do just that. A crowd of other class members gathered around our table to share and share alike. We were all interested to find out just why Dr. Bramlette had invited the back row to stay after class, but we knew we probably would never know.

Jesse showed us his perfect paper. He did have a 100 written in large numbers. Bill, Meg and Jean were proud of their scores. They all got only one wrong but each wrong answer was on a different question.

Jean asked, "Jesse, what is wrong with my answer?"

She handed him her paper. On question five she had written, 'The three ships became separated and went to different ports.'

Jesse explained, "There were only two ships left to return to Portugal because the Santa Maria had been wrecked off Cape Haitien and its timbers were used to build a fortress for the 39 men who would be left behind as there was no room on the remaining two ships for them."

Meg handed Jesse her paper. He saw that she had missed question three. He said,

"You must not have been very interested in the sailor's problems. The correct answer was "They had trouble understanding the natives languages. The other big problem was the loss of the Santa Maria and their having to leave 39 men in a fort built of the timbers from the ship."

Bill missed question two. He had only mentioned food and gold. Jesse reminded him that they had gotten interested in the wild life, both flora and fauna, as well as the crafts of cloth and trinkets.

Chapter 24
A New Schedule

Now it was just two more days until our first outside reading assignments would be shared. We also had the reading of the second chapter to do. Then we would get our second outside reading assignments. We would get our scripts and begin studying our lines for the upcoming production. We were already beginning to feel over worked and under partied. We would just have to work out our schedules to always include 'Bill and Jesse time'.

Bill and Jesse asked what we were doing with the rest of our day. We told them of all our homework and preparation for drama and voice. Jesse sadly said, "Well, Bill, I guess this is about the end of our happy rope. Our girls are becoming too studious."

Bill responded, "Oh, no. We will have to get our schedules adjusted to theirs and still find time to be together. Maybe we could do some of the cooking and relieve them of that chore.

"Now you are talking my kind of talking," answered Jesse. "I believe we can figure out something far better than that. How about we sit right here on this bench and get to it?"

No one wanted to break up their good times and no one wanted to shirk on their studying, either. They sat a quiet minute before looking around to see who would make the first suggestion. We need not to have wondered, It was Jesse, of course.

"How would it be to plan to study at the library some together and then go into town in Bill's car for an occasional meal? Then we guys could buy and prepare two or more evening meals each week. Then if Jean and Meg could do their thing on days they were not in practice, they could do the cooking. What do you think?"

Everyone was deep in thought on his suggestions but not for long. "We can try that and if we need to make adjustments from time to time, we could do that and then go back to Jesse's plan." Meg added.

All of that sound plausible so it was agreed to at least try it out. Jesse then wanted to know if his plan would work for all of us. He suggested, "We can let the girls decide when is best for them to cook and we will decide on the meals uptown and our cooking times."

"Okay, but tonight, it is our turn as we do not have rehearsals today." Jean stated emphatically.

No one objected to her offer so we all went our own ways. Meg and Jean went home and the guys would be elsewhere until nearer mealtime.

It was very pleasant to follow that schedule. It was not too confining for anyone and yet we were together almost as much as we had gotten used to. That was great for all of us.

Fall was settling into the hill country pretty quickly. Gym classes now moved from the great outdoors into the gym and would be there until spring. The drama and music classes were going well. Bill and Jesse had taken on some stage hand jobs and seemed to enjoy doing that. The best times were when they got to hear their girlfriend's beautiful music. They both agreed that both girls were truly blessed with that ability.

As time for the play neared, time became even busier but they still could stick pretty well to their initial plan for meals and time together. Finally, the show "would go on" tomorrow night.

Chapter 25
The New Production

Meg and Jean had performed since childhood but were still excited and anxious to get on with it.

The play was to be performed as a dress rehearsal for the faculty on Wednesday. Then on Friday night it would be for students, parents and anyone else who was interested.

The dress rehearsal was done well . Both Jesse and Bill got to see the entire show for their first time as their jobs had kept them out of the auditorium a lot. Jesse was really impressed with their good work and Bill was , too, but he already really knew how well they could perform.

Jesse and Bill were full of complimentary remarks and the girls thanked them for their special efforts to have everything in exactly the right place for each scene.

Now Friday night would be the proof of the pudding when the students would see the show. They all 'just couldn't wait'.

The following day was exceptionally long but it was restful. No rehearsal. No stage hands needed. Everyone could just relax and enjoy each others company. Having dinner out at a different restaurant was fun, too.

After the final show, the faculty had a real party for the staff and cast. That was sort of expected, but just not to all of that grand style. Many of the faculty had returned to see the final show as had the families of the performers.

Chapter 26
The Family Weekend

Both Meg's and Jean's families were there. They were planning to stay over for the weekend. They had made plans to include both Jesse and Bill. After the show, they all met at Megs and Jean's house for a brief time to work out any kinks in their plan.

The plan was to go on a picnic , weather permitting. If not a picnic, then they would all be together at the girls house all day. They told Jesse and Bill that they really already knew them based on all the information from Meg and Jean. Jesse and Bill informed them that they had been learning about them also and that they would be happy to accept their invitation to hang around.

Mrs. Buckner was not satisfied with that idea. She insisted that they were to be treated as family. The guys were pleased to add, "We'll do our best to fulfill your desires."

That settled, the families left to go to their hotels and the guys went to their dorms. At last, Meg and Jean could each congratulate each others performances. It was finally agreed that their work was about equal and they had fulfilled their roles as 'stars' very well. Then off to bed and an early day tomorrow to serve breakfast for all their guests.

The entire weekend went without a hitch. Everyone was fascinated with all the others in the group and weren't afraid to say so every chance they got. It was all fun and a welcome change of pace from the last few days when everything seemed to all be happening at once.

Late Sunday afternoon, the folk were about to depart to Murphy. Jesse and Bill presented their girl's families with small gifts in very attractively wrapped boxes. The girls insisted that they open them immediately, especially as they had no knowledge about the boy's plans to do that.`

Jesse and Bill said nothing, but they were watching closely to see how the families would respond. They didn't have to wait long. Both Mother's were holding the packages. They each removed the ribbon and opened the boxes. Inside each one, there was a picture of some of the native plants found on campus and a poem about the plants. Everybody wanted to hear the poem and see the picture and then an explanation about their creation.

Bill said, "Jesse is the poet and I tried really hard to not make a complete mess of the plant's pictures."

Everyone was most complimentary toward each man's skill. Meg asked, "How is it that Jean and I didn't know about your talents in this regard?"

Jesse said, "We were purposely keeping that from you, to surprise you."

"The talent is no surprise as you both are so very gifted. I expect you could be asked to design all the programs for our other shows and write poetry to be included in the announcements and brochures."

"And rightly so. You are all gifted in your own ways. Thank you for the gifts and for being such good friends to our daughters."

With that they drove away, leaving very happy folk to get ready for another week of classes.

Chapter 27
Comparing Talents

But first Meg and Jean had to learn more about the poetry and art. Jean went first, "Bill, I have known you for almost two and a half years. How could I not know you could draw?"

Bill answered, "Since I do not doodle all the time and have only used that ability to do class assignments as needed, there have been no occasions to show you any art work that I am capable of doing. Too, I didn't know you were so talented a singer as you have proven to be in the last little while. Why is it that you are not always singing?"

Jean answered, "I just go around doing it in my head and not actually singing. I would think that hearing someone singing as much as I really want to, would be boring."

"Meg, is that what you do , too? Sing in your head instead of aloud?" Jesse quizzed.

Jean asked, "Meg, will you sing something with me? I just can't get it out of my head."

Meg agreed. They began singing with no further ado. The men were very impressed with the ease with which they performed. They both suggested a song title that they especially liked and asked them if they knew it. "We'd love to hear Dixie or The Battle Hymn of the Republic."

The girls immediately sang the first verses of each tune. Now Bill and Jesse were really impressed. They agreed that the girls sounded better without accompaniment than they did with it.

"What are some tunes that are popular these days that you can sing?" they asked.

The girls were getting tired of singing so much when what they really wanted to do was to hear more of Jesse's poetry and see more of Bill's art.

"How about you guys performing more of your skills? Jesse do you remember any of your other poetry?" Meg asked.

"Sure. I can recite it all night if you want." He said.

"No, I don't want you to do that, but say a couple of them for us, please."

His other newest poem was written while in Iraq. It turned out to be quite sad and both girls got teary eyed. Meg asked, "How about a happy one?"

Jesse then said a very long and somewhat comical poem about his childhood. He did it so easily that anyone would have thought he was reading it aloud. He wasn't reading it at all. He repeated it from memory. Jean asked, "Are you remembering from photo or 'phono', memory?"

Jesse explained that the two memories were one and the same.

Both girls were thinking what a joy it would be for them to have been blessed with his phenomenal ability, especially during a time when they were both faced by a new play to memorize the parts for the starring roles.

Bill had been quietly busy for a while with his art on tiny pieces of paper. He seemed to have finished what he had set out to do. He asked, "Are you two lovely ladies ready to see my art work now?"

They had both been so busy with the memory questions that they really were not aware that Bill had been doing anything other than listening to their conversation.

Jean asked, "Do you have something new?"

"I do." he said as he stood up to share them with the girls.

What they saw on paper was such a surprise to them, they were speechless. That in itself was fairly unusual. Their silent awe was even more surprising to Jesse. He asked, "May I see what you two are looking at?"

Neither girl made any response to his question. He asked again, "May I see what Bill has drawn?"

Something seemed to return them to the here and now. They both held up the tiny papers that Bill had given them. Jesse caught a glimpse of their faces on the paper. He too, was quite impressed with what little he had gotten to see before the girls each went over to hug Bill. Jean also gave him a big kiss.

"I really need to see what Bill had done to that paper. When am I going to get my hands on them?" Jesse pleaded.

By this time, Bill was dancing Jean around the room. Meg shared her picture with him. "I see what you girls mean. That shows a very deep seated talent. It's a shame he has only done school assignments with it, until now."

Bill's and Jean's dance ended as suddenly as it had begun. Bill said, "I appreciate all of your enjoyment based on my talented pencil , but it is no more wondrous than the talent each of you have exhibited."

His statement seemed to put all of them on the same plane of abilities. They in turn made brief statements about their perception. "Oh, but we had to learn our talent the hard way. You folks were born with yours," Meg stated emphatically.

"Oh, no you don't. You know we had to try and try again before we mastered our talents. We, too, did not do this from birth."

A few more kudos, hugs and kisses were shared before the men took their leave to return to their dorms. After they left, Meg and Jean, sat down on the sofa and shared their picture? with each other. They decided that each one was equally well done. And that was really, really well done!!

Jean asked, "Do you think we will ever get to sleep tonight? How will we be able to turn out the lights? That will mean that we could no longer see Bills exceptional art work."

They had hardly taken their eyes off the picture Bill had given each of them. They turned on more light and sat nearer to its glow than they had been earlier. This really got them excited even more, They knew that he had done these exquisite portraits very quickly. "He must have begun on them after our discussion with Jesse about his memory. That couldn't have been more than five minutes." Jean stated.

Meg nodded her head affirmatively and said, "Yes, that is part of what makes them so very precious, don't you think?"

Jean added, "Maybe he has practiced doing this before. That would enable him to have completed then so very quickly. Either way, I will treasure it forever."

Meg agreed wholeheartedly, saying, "You bet!! I will always treasure this."

Chapter 28
Christmas Break

Classes resumed and the foursome kept each others company regularly over the coming weeks and months. The wintry winds arrived.

Their production of the new play had been busy but enjoyable. Bill and Jesse were still doing some work at the theater. Bill's talent had been shown to be exquisite and he was asked to do the brochures for their next productions.

All of that came to a screeching halt with the advent of Christmas break. There had been a lot of news articles written about their show, 'White Christmas'. They had been all about the entire caste and all of the support groups.

All of the foursome returned to their own homes. The girls went to Murphy. Jesse and Bill went home to their family's farms. That is, for a few days. Then there were phone calls made to arrange visits at the homes of the girls. That way, the four would all get to be together the rest of the time in Murphy..

Meg's and Jean's families and friends met the guys, welcoming them into their homes and churches, Meg and Jean were to perform some Christmas music during the services that weekend. They knew the music already, so that helped give them time to thoroughly enjoy every minute of Bill's and Jesse's visit.

The planned visit included all of the days until college classes began again. The weather was particularly appropriate for all of their days out of doors in the snow. Jean and Meg had never skied or snowboarded before. Both Bill and Jesse had and they were good teachers. The girls innate athletic abilities set them in good stead to be able to learn swooshing downhill in the snow in other ways than on a sled, as they had done in their childhood.

Chapter 29
Jesse's New Plan

Like all other good things, the holiday came to a halt and school began again. They all happily bade their families and/or their new found friends farewell in order to get back to school. All seemed to be so right with their worlds and the return to the routine of school was welcomed and life went on.

Jesse registered for the ultimate limit of classes that anyone could register for. He had decided that he would somehow graduate with Bill, Jean and Meg even if they were two whole years ahead of him. They were all Juniors. He was a Freshman.

He had requested some help from his teachers and the registrar in order to attempt that feat. It was almost unheard of, and surely not known of at WCU. He would have to take extra classes each semester and do summer school or on line classes which were just coming into vogue. He really thought it could be done. His friends all believed in him, too.

It became necessary for him to spend a bit more time on his school work than before but he managed and came out smelling like a rose, all A's on all his subjects.

They all missed American History at eight o'clock Monday, Wednesday and Friday, but they had worked out schedules so that they almost spent as much time together as before. None of them wanted to cut back on dating.

Meg's and Jean's new schedule was a bit easier to manage without theatrical productions. Bill and Jesse still had some classes together but Jesse spent no more time on projects than before Christmas.

Chapter 30
The Party with the Surprise Ending

Jeans' and Meg's door was often open to their friends other than just Bill and Jesse. They planned a party in February for Valentine's Day. They had had their plans made for that over their Christmas break. Their parents were going to bring a lot of the refreshments and stay at a motel while visiting their daughters.

The party was fun but not quite as much fun as the birthday party last fall. The crowd was not diminished and the appetites held up miraculously.

Their decor was hearts and flowers. After the party, when all the guests had left except for Jesse and Bill, Meg and Jean sensed something else was afoot, but they could not figure it out. No one was saying anything differently but there was an undercurrent that caused some speculation to take over.

Bill said, "Jean, would you go with me for a drive?"

Jean accepted and got her coat. Jesse and Meg seemed to be going to stay put.

After Jean and Bill left, Jesse took Meg into his arms, planted one of his best kisses on her lips and fell onto one knee. He looked up at her and said, "Will you marry me?"

Meg took no more than a moment to say, "Yes."

Jesse slipped a diamond on her finger and continued to hold her close.

Jean and Bill had driven down to the bend in the river near the island on the back side of the hill the University was built upon. He stopped the car, got out, came around to her side of the car, opened the door, took her hand in his, pulled her out of the car, took her into his arms and said, "Will you marry me?"

It wasn't even a moment before she said, "Yes."

Bill slipped a diamond onto her finger and continued to hold his dearest one close.

They then reentered the car, looked deeply into each others eyes, and began to realize that a new life was at hand.

A deep discussion ensued. Bill had a lot to say and Jean listened quietly for a while. Then she began to talk just as seriously as Bill had. There was really going to be some changes in their life's plans, beginning now.

Their talk seemed to have no end until Bill said, "I suppose that Jesse and Meg are doing just what we are doing."

That was an enlightening statement that brought Jean back to her usual level of sensibility. She asked, "Do you mean that Jesse is asking her the same question that you asked me?"

"Yes, that is exactly what the plan included. We have been in love for months. School has taken more of our time, especially with Jesse taking a load and a half. No one could do that except him that I know. Don't you just love to watch him accomplish so much so easily?"

Jean said, "Jesse insisted that there was no way to attain his colossal ability except to have been born with it. Yet, I feel that it is rubbing off on all of us. I feel that I can do some things with more ease and remember things longer than I used to be able to do. Don't you?"

Bill nodded his head affirmatively. "Yes, now that you mention it, I believe so. I have been able to read things only once and am able to better retain what I have read. Is that sort of what you mean?"

"I really do believe that. I do not have to refer so often to recipes that I have used over and over. I don't have to struggle to remember where I put things like I used to. Meg has mentioned it often of late. It has been affecting all of us without our really knowing it."

Bill checked his watch and asked if Jean agreed that it was time to head back to her house. She agreed and soon they were back in the driveway at home.

Both got out of the car and arm in arm walked to the door. On their first step onto the porch, the front door flew open and two happy friends came out to greet them.

Then they all fell silent. Who would speak first? Jean just couldn't wait to hear their news and to tell her's and Bill's news. She said, "Are you two engaged, too?"

Meg squealed and said, "Does that mean you two are also engaged?"

They all joined hands and skipped in a circle until they feared they would be awakening their neighbors. That quietened them all down so they withdrew to the house to continue their merriment more quietly indoors.

Bill said, "Oh, I almost forgot." as he retraced his footsteps out to his car. He returned with a bottle of champagne.

That sent Jean and Meg to the sideboard to get goblets. They were soon making toasts to their futures. It had been a spectacular evening. A never to be forgotten evening if there ever was to be such a thing.

Soon the guys left to go back to their dorms. Jean and Meg settled down for one of their long, long talks. They were planning the rest of their lives and just couldn't stop until the sun started coming up.

Chapter 31
Now Everyone Knows

How were they to be able to function normally today? Oh well. They didn't have to get dressed so they would have time to get some breakfast before their classes would begin.

Meg asked. "What will our friends think and say when they see our rings?"

Jean said, "They will all be happy for us. Let's get started on our way to the auditorium." Their first classes each day of the week were in the auditorium. They were practicing for just one production this term.

When they arrived, the very first of their friends asked, "Do you have some news for us?"

Jean asked, "Why do you ask?"

"From the looks of those shiners on your third fingers, left hand, we thought you just might have some news to share." they replied.

More joyous frolicking ensued. With the arrival of their professor who couldn't help but overhear their gladsome voices, there were still more questions asked as to why the merriment. When one of their friends said, "Meg and Jean have news for you."

The girls both displayed their ring fingers. The instructors offered their congratulations and then wanted to get down to the business at hand.

That was just the beginning of the celebrations of that momentous day. Jean and Meg forgot they had had no sleep last night and that allowed their day to progress for them, more or less normally.

When their morning classes ended, Meg and Jean headed home. Before they arrived, they heard rapid footsteps behind them. They turned to see Bill and Jesse about to catch up with them. More excitement!!

The foursome proceeded on to the girl's house. There were just enough leftovers form the party for their lunches. Jesse had to leave first for one of his extra classes. The others rested and talked about their new found relationships. All was joyous and highly unusual. Bill asked, "Will we always feel like this?'"

Jean assured him that she certainly hoped so. He agreed and grinned from ear to ear. That caused Jean to be a bit curious. What could he possibly have on his mind now.

He continued, "Love is a 'many splendered thing'. At least so I have heard. I do hope that is a true statement."

Jean went over to sit on his lap. Meg left the room to her two dear friends. She was keeping up with the time while she was doing things in her room to make it more normal looking. She stepped out of her room to tell Jean and Bill that it was almost time for their next classes. They were gone. Then she heard them on the porch. The cold weather could not even staunch their joy.

They all were soon ready to face their afternoon classes. Bill had gym and they had voice lessons. They parted their ways and were off to class.

After classes were over, the four met at the snack shop as per usual. There was more celebration as their news got around. More congratulations and joy in each other.

Chapter 32
A Really Big Snow Storm

The weather outside became frightful when snow began to fall. Jesse still had a class and conference with the registrar. The others were trying to decide what they could be doing in Jesse's absence. Meg grinned from ear to ear as she started suggesting that the three of them, go home to their house and prepare supper for all of them. Bill thought that that would be fun. He wasn't much of a cook, but he could run errands and eat when the food was ready.

They sloshed through the snow drifts as they traveled homeward. When they arrived, Jean and Meg checked the fridge and pantry. What they found was almost total emptiness. There was almost nothing they could do with only chicken dressing, cans of salmon, no bread and and nothing sweet.

They moved toward the living room and heard Jesse,cleaning his shoes. That must have been a shortened class or something. They had not as yet gotten dinner planned, let alone prepared.

Jesse had news. The roads were all closed in their area. The college staff had held a meeting by phone as no one could drive and they certainly didn't want to be walking in that blizzard. They had decided to cancel classes today since there were so many students who lived off campus.

Meg and Jean just couldn't think about what that would mean for them, They lived off campus but very near to the campus, maybe a half block away. They were getting scared that they would not be able to get food from the store.

Bill suggested that they make a list of the things they would need to get. He would walk to the nearest store to get whatever they needed.

Meg said, "Maybe we could all go to get the groceries and help to carry it home." Jesse suggested , "We might need to phone the grocer to see if he is still open."

A brief phone call assured them that they just might be open for business all night. Jean had been in the kitchen writing a list. They all got their outer wear on and started to the store. It was surprising to learn that a big crowd was out shopping. They hoped they could get waited on before the store shelves became empty.

They had sloshed through the falling snow that had already accumulated about eight inches, they still saw some cars on the streets but they were moving slowly or not at all. There was a lot of traffic on foot. On arriving at the grocery store, they were not surprised to find a lot of folk had arrived before them.

The fellows decided to wait outside while the girls selected the groceries. That way, there would be at least two fewer people in their way.

Jean and Meg had gotten into the habit of writing their lists of groceries in the order they would be found when moving from aisle to aisle. Their progress was slower then usual, but steady. About 30 minutes had passed when they stepped out the door, laden with too many bags. Jesse and Bill rushed to their aid. When all had been divided, the foursome started back to the house to prepare supper.

There was much slipping and sliding, but soon they had arrived on the deck. Meg unlocked the door. Once inside where it was warm, they all went straight to the kitchen to unload the makings for their supper.

Jean said, "Let's all put our bags on the floor over near the pantry." That done, Meg and Jean started putting all the items in their proper places except those that were to be used tonight. They put those things on the shelf beside the sink. Bill emptied the bags and Jesse opened the cans, got out the pots and pans needed, and began cooking. Bill started on the salad while the girls finished their tasks. With their team effort, supper was ready in almost no time at all. The table had been set, the food was served and all gathered around the table to enjoy eating and visiting.

They had all agreed that the trip to the store had gone well, and now they were enjoying the fruits of their labors.

Meg remarked, "I believe that that is the quickest we have ever achieved all that effort, and I think we should pause and give thanks to God for all of his help."

Jean asked, "Who will lead us in the blessing?"

Bill said, "I will. Let us bow our heads."

He began with, 'Our Father, who art in heaven, bless this food to the nourishment of our bodies and also the many hands that prepared it. This we ask for Jesus sake, Amen."

All the rest added, "Amen."

The food was soon served, eaten with gusto, and with the merriment of good conversation, all was finished and then they were faced with the prospect of cleanup. Jesse made his offer, "I'll wash the dishes if the rest of you put all this away."

That was the usual solution for clearing away all semblance of their meals together. When all were finished, they gathered in the living room to cuddle and visit. Jean suggested, "Let's play a game."

Their was no need to ask, 'What game?' They all enjoyed playing gin rummy. Soon the cards were on the dining table and all four gathered around the table to enjoy an evening of it.

In what seemed like a very short time, Bill happened to glance at his watch. He was surprised to find it was so late. He said, "My, how time flies when you're having fun. Can you believe that it is 12 o'clock?"

Since they all had eight o'clock classes, their departure was swift, either to go back to dorms, or to settle down in their own room right here.

They all kissed goodnight, and rushed off to their destinations. Meg and Jean found themselves in bed very shortly. Lights were turned off and sleep overtook them, Bill and Jesse had a brief hike up a mountain before arriving at their dorm.

They waved goodby and they, too, were soon asleep.

Chapter 33
Goody, Goody Gout, Schools Out

Time marched on, classes were attended, assignments were done, friends were entertained, families were kept informed as to their progress, Productions were performed, dating continued as per usual. Jesse did all the required work for all of his regular classes and also for his additional classes. All was happy and nice.

Before they knew it, the school year came to an end. The girls went home to Murphy. Bill went home to his family farm. Jesse signed up for summer school and for some more on line classes.

All four of them were together every weekend either in Murphy or at WCU. Their families were as interested in their schedules as the four of them were. Before they knew what had happened, it was time to register for the fall classes of their last year in college. Jesse would be able to graduate with Bill, Meg and Jean. Life was good.

The foursome dug in and mastered whatever came their way. Meg and Jean had three productions this year. One in the Fall and two in the Spring. Jesse was well on his way to be the next Head of the Class in the spring.

Dr. Bramlette kept in touch with them by phone and in person at the Snack Shop.

Bill was being sought out to illustrate all sorts of things for very good prices. At first he was hesitant to accept very many offers but none of them took a lot of his time and the money in the bank looked very good to him.

Meg and Jean were to try out for the solo parts in a production by a well known group in Asheville. Jesse didn't have very much time to write poetry but he managed to get some off to publishers twice in his last year in college. It was well received and much appreciated by the readers. He received some pretty good checks.

The Asheville musical group sent their music to a bigger organization with their approval. It was well received and the bigger group wanted them to be available after graduation in May.

All of their plans somehow worked out and they fulfilled all that was asked of them. Their bank accounts were being well fed.

Their one problem that was very difficult to overcome, was that they had too little time for each other. They had started doing their meals together all the time in the cafeteria. Bill could draw and visit at the same time. That made the others jealous as they could not practice music and date, too. Nor could Jesse write poetry when any of those three were with him. Besides, he almost met himself coming back every time he stepped out side his dorm room.

Were they all happy? Duh. That was the motion that kept their world spinning. They were each there for the others anytime, anywhere.

Chapter 34
Graduation and Wedding

The last day of classes was the day before graduation. Their classes were over but the girls were having a hard time with all the changes that had occurred and that lay ahead. Graduation was a bit hectic, at first. Being fitted for caps and gowns was only a small part of it.

All of their friends were hovering about, willing to do whatever was needed to assist them in their final preparations for the biggest week in their lives. Jesse was to speak at graduation. He was graduating Magna Cum Laude. Everybody in the state, not just at WCU, were in awe of him and his innate abilities. He had accomplished a most impossible feat in doing four years of college in two years and a summer school instead of the usual four years required for those of us who are normal. Of course he also took classes on the internet, too.

Bill had been especially busy while drawing some of the artwork needed for the graduation ceremony. Heretofore, the college had bought that sort of thing from their usual supplier. He was more than happy to get to do it and did his usual exceptional job.

Meg and Jean were in the chorus but they had been excused from performing during graduation. That was a much needed break as they had a lot of other things on their minds. They were to graduate and then get married two days later. Much of the planning and preparation had been done for them by their mothers and other members of their families. They had made a trip to Asheville to shop for their wedding dresses.

They both liked the same design at first, but finally decided it would be best to have different styles. They did that ,by neither of them getting their favorite but a substitute for each that were very different.

Meg's dress was off shoulder and very bouffant with tiny sequins on the bodice. Jean chose one that was softly draped in both the bodice and the skirt. They seemed to compliment each other. Their headdress was a problem for them to settle on since they neither liked to wear things on their head other than in rainy or snowy weather. Meg happened to see a tiara that looked good on her, Jean asked if she could try it. They decided to each wear the same style. They were quite happy with their choices and had a hard time not showing them to Bill and Jesse.

The bridesmaids all chose the same dress but in different colors The men would all wear tuxedos. Everybody liked the idea of having the wedding before noon. The time was set at 11:00 AM with a reception following in the cafeteria. The cafeteria staff had asked if they might host the party. Their offer was gratefully accepted. They would be served a buffet that would serve as lunch and refreshments.

The college had never had a wedding and reception after graduation before but they seemed to like all of the formality and the lingering of so many students. The foursome's parents and other family members were glad to have some of the planning taken off their shoulders.

All in all, the day turned out perfectly. The weather was spectacular. The chaplain and the music staff of the university had taken on the service and the music. It was all splendid. By late afternoon, the newlyweds were ready to drive off into the sunset, but in different cars. Jesse's gift from his family was a car. All four members of the wedding party slipped off to change into street clothes so that their families could take the formal wear home for them.

Chapter 35
The Honeymoons Begin

When the cars left the parking lot, they had been beautifully decorated with old shoes and tin cans, streamers and banners. They were quite a sight as they sped out of sight.

The rest of the wedding party said their farewells and started home after a very busy week. They were all happy for their newly married sons and daughters.

Meg and Jean had not shared their honeymoon destinations. Bill and Jesse had not shared, either. They all were surprised that the car behind was still following the one ahead. They had hoped that the cans and shoes would just all fall off and get left behind. But no, they seemed to stay put, so both cars stopped to rid themselves of the stuff.

Both couples were full of joy and happiness for themselves and for their dearest friends. There was a strange look passed around as they all returned to their cars. When they started off, they were still going the same direction. That seemed odd to all of them but they just kept on driving.

When they needed to stop for dinner, the lead car waited until the followers were inside the restaurant before they reentered their car and left. Jesse had decided that he was tired of being followed.

Jean and Bill wondered what was taking Jesse and Meg so long to get into the restaurant. They soon forgot about everyone except each other. They enjoyed their dinner and left in quite a leisurely fashion.

When they got underway again, Bill asked, "Do you know where they are going tonight?"

Jean said, "No, I haven't a clue. But I can't wait to get to the beach where we can relax and enjoy each other."

"I agree one hundred percent. It has been a while since we have seen the broad Atlantic. I am glad we are staying in that lodge on the beach, aren't you?" Bill asked.

Jean said, "Oh, I don't know, anywhere with you will be perfect for the rest of our lives."

Bill thought about that for a moment before he said, "Don't you think it would be better to stop at a motel along the way for the night and finish the drive tomorrow?"

"It will be quite late before we can drive all the way to the beach. Now that you mention it, I think stopping would be a good idea. In fact, we just passed a very attractive motel just now." Jean added.

"Then you agree that stopping for the night will be okay?" Bill asked as he slowed down to make the turn to go back to that motel he, too, had noticed.

When they were about to find a parking spot at the motel, Bill recognized Jesse's new car. He said, "Can you believe that Meg and Jesse are stopping here, too? Do you want to go in or go somewhere else?"

Jean answered, "Do you think we have been with them so long and so closely associated, that we still are just automatically making the same decisions? What the heck. Let's stop here, too."

When they entered the motel office, they expected to see Jesse and Meg. They weren't there. They went ahead and signed in, got their luggage, and entered the main entrance to the rooming area. They weren't anywhere in sight. As they proceeded down the hall to their room, a man came out of the door next to the one they were looking for. It was Jesse. They hugged each other and asked about Meg. She heard them and joined in the fun.

They all started laughing. Jean got her voice back first and asked, "Is this truly a joke or are we just so in tune with each other that we are still thinking alike?"

Jesse could speak at last, "I think we are just about the closest friends I have ever known. We are heading to the Atlantic Ocean and Morehead City. Where are you bound for?"

All were nodding their heads while they were laughing so hard they couldn't talk. Bill spoke first. "We would save some money if we took only one car. That is where we are going."

Jesse agreed. He said, "I'm game if you two are."

Meg said, "We have done everything together for two years. Why not honeymoon together....up to a point?"

Bill asked, "Jean, what do you have to say about this brand new idea?"

"I think it will be more fun together, don't you?" she responded.

"Okay, let's get settled in and see each other at breakfast in the morning." Jesse suggested.

Everybody agreed. The two doors were closed and the most wonderful evening followed.

Chapter 36
Second Day of the Honeymoon

Next morning, they knew when their neighbors were up and taking showers by the noise from the adjacent room. Everyone finished about the same time. Now they had to decide where they should have breakfast. Meg and Jean went down to the dining room in the motel and found it to their liking. They had told their men to follow if they didn't come right back. Just moments passed before Jesse and Bill entered and found the girls as they were being seated near the windows.

"Did everybody get enough rest? Jean asked,

Bill said, "I don't think I did. We have run at a hectic pace for days now. It's beginning to catch up with me. It will be good to lie on the beach and watch the waves and the scudding clouds. Maybe then, I will get some much needed rest."

Jesse added, "After my speechifying yesterday, I was worn out. Now after the wedding and the long drive, I think I will need some more R&R, too."

Meg had been unusually quiet. She finally said, "I suppose all of us are both physically and emotionally exhausted. But I have never been happier."

The rest indicated that they felt the very same way. Jean started thinking aloud. "We will be together at the beach. Then we will have to return to WCU to claim our things before going on to Asheville to find suitable lodging. Both Meg and I will have to report to work as soon as we arrive there. Our singing with that traveling troupe for the next several months will give Jesse and Bill some time to decide on just what they want to do next. Of course they will continue creating poetry and art work in their spare time unless they find a job in engineering. If that was to come about, we will all have to find semi-permanent homes somewhere in the area."

"You've got that right. I have been thinking about just how all that will work out for us." Bill said

Meg had been noticing the housing that seemed available for rent that she had observed along the road. Meg idly mused, "I have been window shopping about that as we drove along. I have noticed a lot of two family homes. Do you think that would be a good idea while we are feeling our way into the future?"

Jesse and Bill neither spoke for a bit. Then Jesse said, "If that is what you two lovely ladies want to do, it's fine with me........ for a while. What do you think, Bill?"

Bill usually left the decisions up to Meg, Jean and Jesse, but this time he spoke up quite vehemently. "I think I wouldn't have it any other way."

After their stopover night at the motel on the way to the beach, they now needed to find breakfast and move on toward the beach. Jesse asked,"Are we going to park one car and continue on together?"

With no hesitation, the others agreed. Bill said, "Jesse's car is roomier than mine, Shall we ride with Jesse and Meg and leave our car here somewhere?"

Jesse suggested, "We might ask for advise as to where to park the extra car. Driving mine on will be fine, if Bill will do some of the driving."

Jesse spied a building with a sign out front that said, Long Term Parking Available. They stopped and found that that lot was under watchful eyes 24/7. It would be the perfect place to stash an extra car while the travelers continued on together.

Finally they were underway again in Jesse's car. It was really good that all the luggage would fit in his trunk.

Bill and Jesse took turns driving. Miles sped by. Conversations were happy and time flew. They were already seeing sea gulls. The beach couldn't be far, now.

On arriving at the lodge on the beach, both couples decided to take a walk on the beach before settling in for the night. They did chose to go in opposite directions. It was lovely to walk beneath the starry sky with the sound of waves crashing on the beach.

They must have walked about the same distance before returning to the lodge. They returned to the car at almost the same time. Jesse opened his trunk to allow everyone to claim their luggage. Then they filed in to register. They were welcomed by a surprise. Some of their friends from school had phoned ahead to order a really nice nightcap and something to eat to be ready for them. They were all puzzled as to just how they had known where they were all going.

After some discussion, they all realized that they had all mentioned their destination to several friends. They figured that the friends had all learned about it and pitched in to make their arrival especially interesting. They would have to get more thank you notes to write to them and all the others who had been so supportive.

Both couples had reserved rooms in different parts of the lodge. Maybe they were not always destined to think exactly alike after all.

Their four days flew by. All of it was happy and full of fun. After packing Jesse's trunk once again, they drove back to pick up Bill's car and then drive on to the University. Bill and Jean wanted to shop at a huge mall where they found some really special thank you cards to send to their friends while Jesse and Meg just sat on a bench nearby until Bill and Jean returned.

Chapter 37
The Return to the Real World

The shoppers returned and they headed west.

Once back at WCU, they found summer school to be in session. The summer school students appeared to all be strangers. The honeymooner's were ready to reclaim their worldly goods which they found would require at least one trailer to take all of their accumulated items to Asheville. Bill had a hitch already, so his car was elected to tow the rented trailer. Soon all were underway again. This time the trailer slowed Bill and Jean down. Jesse and Meg found a place to eat a late meal before driving further. While parked there, Jean spotted their car and she and Bill stopped in, also.

Both men were tired of driving but they had the trailer loaded and were uneasy about parking it overnight. It was decided to call ahead to see if a couple of men friends of Jesse's and Bill's would be willing to share their house with them for the night. They of course were eager to see them again and hear about their latest adventures. They hoped that they remembered correctly that a large garage stood behind that house where their trailer could be housed safely.

Chuck and Jim were former students at WCU. They had found jobs quickly and moved in together. While the visitors were talking and looking around, they kept seeing beautiful pictures of two girls scattered about. Bill asked. "Chuck what can tell us about your decorative photos."

Chuck grinned, and said, "I have been wondering when someone would ask us about that. Jim, shall we tell our guests about Ginny and Angie?"

Jim said, "Sure. You go first."

Chuck picked up a couple of photos of one of the girls. He said, "This in Angie, We have been dating a couple of years. We are planning to marry in September after she and Ginny get finished with their work at the summer camp for Girl Scouts near here. Now Jim, it's your time."

"Well, my plans have not moved along as quickly as Chuck's. Ginny is going to take some more classes to get her re'sume' up to snuff. After that, Ginny and I will be married,too."

After a good visit, the men said they would have to get on to bed as they were scheduled to be at work at 6:00 AM tomorrow.

Jesse said, "That's great. We'll get up early, too, and leave at the same time. We can't thank you enough for storing our trailer for us until we find a place to unload it in Asheville."

Both Chuck and Jim said there was no need for us to rush off. And yes , the trailer would be safe until we needed to get it.

Bill said, "An early start would be a good idea anyway. We have a lot to take care of in Asheville. Meg and Jean are to begin their jobs tomorrow. Jesse and I have to find some work before long in order to support these lovely brides in the manor they are accustomed. Too, the really big job is finding affordable housing"

Everybody did get a good night's sleep and were ready to get on to Asheville early next morning.

Chapter 38
On to Asheville

All of them had been to Asheville on numerous occasions to see shows that were traveling through. Bill and Jesse would visit some realtors to make arrangements for all of them to see some houses after the girls returned from work.

It was getting on toward noon before they found a realtor who had duplexes . They were greeted congenially and then they got right down to the business of finding something quickly. The lady at the first desk had some houses built for two families. She had several pictures and their addresses. Price was important to the young men, so they made sure they were talking about something that would be affordable. They asked for an appointment to see some of the houses after 2:15 PM.

They got in touch with the girls in time to meet the realtors at the duplexes. They were all excited to be seeing their prospective homes together. The map was easy to follow. They arrived just after the realtor. The outside of the first house was not very attractive even though it had a bright shiny new coat of paint. They looked it over and found that there were other things not to their collective liking.

They followed the realtor to the next house. Right away they were remarking about the vast differences between it and the first one. The girls were looking at the windows and the shrubs. The men were looking at the way the house had been engineered. All of them were eager to look inside.

The inside was even more interesting than the outside. The floor plan was very much like their house at the edge of campus where they had spent so much time together. There were apartments exactly alike. Each had two bedrooms, a living room, a kitchen and dining room, and a porch. The men were asking questions as to when it was constructed, the manufacturer of the heat pump, the ownership and just how it came to be on the market. The salesman had most of their necessary info on paper, but he also knew some other information that they were interested in, also.

Meg and Jean were eying the windows, the closets, the storage space in the kitchen, the appliances, and were asking about carpets and floor coverings that were in place.

Both couples were quite pleased with the house . It was time to get to the bottom line and sign the papers, set up their mortgage and get moved in.

The realtor was most helpful. While the men took care of the purchasing, the girls went to the furniture store that had been selected to purchase the other necessary furniture. The furniture they had used at college was enough for one of the apartments, but more was needed. They had already decided to get bigger beds, another set of dressers ,another dining room suite and another set of living room furniture. They found that that store would take the twin beds and reduce the overall cost. Too, the bill would be equally divided. That way both couples would have some of their used furniture and also some new furniture.

When all four of them met back at the house that would soon be their new home, they found that all was settled with the mortgage. They had the house keys to prove it. The girls had found that the furniture could be delivered tomorrow.

In the meantime, they returned to their friend's house to spend one more night. Everyone was still too tired to want to go to a movie or anything else after their dinner, so they just settled down for the night and rested.

Bill and Jesse were interested in job hunting now that they had a home to live in.

They were discussing their schedule of appointments with possible employers, tomorrow. Meg and Jean just showered and fell into bed. They were sleeping so soundly, they didn't know when their husbands joined them. All were quite ready to face a new day when morning came.

Jean and Meg took Jesse's car to their workplace. Bill and Jesse towed the trailer to their new home.

It had been discussed at length just what cleaning would be necessary. Bill and Jesse had bought a new vacuum cleaner and mop jointly to be used by both the new householders. When they unlocked their homes, they decided that they would each work together to clean each dwellings before moving any furniture in.

After a couple of hours of backbreaking sweeping and mopping, both men needed a break and they were very hungry. After locking their cleaning tools in their new homes along with any dirt that had not yet been eliminated, the men went to find a fast food establishment. Once there, they satisfied their hunger and planned the next step in settling in.

Bill said, "What do you think we should do outside the house?"

"Pull weeds, mow, sweep driveway, walks and porches, trim shrubbery, and plant some herbs and tomatoes." answered Jesse.

"That may have to wait until tomorrow or maybe later. If we get both houses clean enough to suit the girls and get our things moved in, we will have accomplished a mountain of chores. Then the girls will probably need help in hanging blinds, curtains, drapes, etc. When will we get on with finding our jobs?" Bill asked.

"Meg and Jean will soon be home. They will get the new furniture delivered. By the way, have you checked at your bank to find the status of your bank account?" Jesse wanted to know.

"I am pretty sure it is still okay. We have both been fortunate in getting paid to do that which we love to do in our spare time, drawing and writing poetry." Bill answered.

"Mine is okay, for now, but it will be crying for a refill soon. Let's get back to the cleaning now. That way, we will be more available to carry furniture and the rest of what is on the trailer into the house. Meg and Jean have been planning big time to clean all the appliances and shelving in storage spaces and to spray disinfectant in sinks and bathrooms. Do you think they will be up to all that today?"

Jesse said, "Never under estimate just what they can do. They have shown us over and over what great housekeeping skills they possess."

"I know all about that. I guess my question was, Will they be up to it after a day of rehearsals?"

"From past experience, I would say that they will both come through with flying colors." Jesse responded.

Bill and Jesse had barely gotten out of their car before Meg and Jean drove in.

They all filled in the blank on their separate activities and came to a consensus of opinion that, 'Now is the time to finish the job.'

Meg and Jean complimented their guys on their good cleaning jobs. They all sat on the edge of the porch to decide just what each should be doing next.

Meg and Jean had been entirely involved in thinking furniture. The things of the trailer were primarily theirs. They listed on paper, the item to be put in Jesse's and Meg's half of the house and the rest would be put in Bill's and Jean's half. They also listed the new furnishings that would go into Jesse's and Meg's house and the rest would go into Bill's and Jean's half.

While the guys were doing that, with occasional help from the girls, the girls would each be cleaning their own appliances, etc. The girls last big job would be to go grocery shopping. They had had almost nothing except cleaning supplies to bring from school. They would need all the basics and some regular groceries.

All got to work and never a cross word was said, or even thought. Home began to look more and more like home to all of them. Then the guys found some telephone wires and jacks that just needed to be reconnected to the cities telephone servers.

They called the phone office and were thrilled to find that a truck would be out to make that connection.

The furniture was in place, all the cleaning finished, the blinds hung, and the kitchen items were in place. Next, the grocery shopping needed to be done and then they would eat out to celebrate and then get some much needed rest in their own homes.

Everyone was too tired to dance about and celebrate but their expressions were exuding, Good Will to All!!!!

Finally they were done and very very happy about all that they had accomplished

To get to spend their first night, "At Home", was the answer to all their prayers.

Now was the time to make those belated calls to all of their homes.

They had not talked with their parents since the wedding, therefore it was decided that some phone calls would be in order. They decided they would take turns calling home to their families. They could do it in ABC order: Bill, Jean, Jesse, and Meg.

Bill phoned his family to tell them their news and find out how they were all getting along. They would all take notes of their family's news to be shared when all the calls were completed.

No one was to share this information until all four calls were made. The phoning moved right along. Some calls were longer than others but none were too long.

When all calls were finished, everyone had exciting and interesting news to share.

Bill went first. He said, "All is well at home. They are all glad to hear from me and to learn how our new ways of living are working out. I told them about the beach, the new digs, and the possibilities for employment in Asheville. They told me that they would be sending money by Western Union to help with our current expenses. They didn't say how much money."

Jesse, Jean and Meg just sat glancing around at each other. They just couldn't believe that Bill's news had been repeated by their families, too. All of their families were sending money by way of Western Union now that we had an address to send it to.

But they would tell their share of that kind of news when it came their time to report. Each of the others reported their family's news and all had received an offer of money to be sent by Western Union.

Jesse said, "I think all of our families have been very generous. They must have made this plan at the wedding. We will have to show them how very grateful we all are. But we will all have to help plan just how to go about that."

Bill and Jesse had written their re'sume's and were getting a list of places to send them. In the meantime they would continue working on things here at home and reading the ads in the newspapers. After all they had just celebrated their first week of marriage on Thursday. They figured they had completed a lot of work in just ten days.

Meg and Jean would be going out of town for the weekend next week to sing in South Carolina. They all knew ahead of time that their music would require some time on the road. A troupe was a traveling affair but this troupe was only doing short, one or two day trips. There was one week long engagement in the fall when the troupe would be visiting colleges and universities to perform.

From now on, their meals would all be cooked and eaten at home . Of course for lunch, the menu was sandwiches until their job would include a lunch break. Besides, the men could fend for themselves some of the time.

Chapter 39
SLOW – MEN WORKING?????

That was a long two days when Meg and Jean were away on their first trip out of town. Too, the men were getting antsy about hearing from their job searches. When the mail was delivered Saturday, there were some letters for each of them. The letters were opened and read immediately. Some letters said no jobs were currently available. There were letters that invited an appointment to be made in the near future, There were some letters that may as well have been printed in gold because they were pretty sure there was work available right her in Buncombe County.

They read and reread the letters. Sorted and resorted the letters. Then, since the girls weren't home, they had nothing better to do than to continue reading them.

They both got some letters from the same companies. They discussed just what that might mean for each of them.

Bill started the conversation. He said, "I have a letter here from the North Carolina DOT. Did you get one like it?"

Jesse nodded affirmatively while he was locating it. They were not just carbon copies, instead they seemed to have been written by two different people. They decided that was a plus for them.

Jesse asked if Bill had received a letter from a local industry. Bill said, "Yes, I have one from Enka, one from a paper mill in Canton, and one from ISB. What local industries did you hear from?"

They found they had received all of the same ones. Of course, both men knew about the other's special abilities concerning engineering. Bill could hold his own pretty well when he and Jesse were discussing any particular kind of engineering job. Jesse thought that Bill was better at some of the skills than he was, but Bill always thought of Jesse's photographic memory. Bill truly believed that Jesse would ultimately get the better job and the most pay. They didn't discuss that element very often.

Jesse thought that now would be a good time to bring up that very subject. He put aside his mail and thoughtfully asked, "Bill, out of all those responses you received, which job seems the most appealing to you?"

Bill thoughtfully answered, "I believe there are several that I could do, but probably not as well as you could do them."

Jesse didn't answer immediately. He finally asked, "Bill, why do you always put yourself down when comparing our abilities?"

Bill had to think a bit before he said, "You have that marvelous memory that never forgets anything you see or hear. That has to be a real asset when designing anything from a dam to a dirt path."

"Bill, you can do math problems more quickly than I can, most of the time. Please stop putting yourself down. And your drawing is superb."

Bill answered, "Okay. I'll try, but my hope is that both of us will get jobs we are really capable of doing, and get them quickly."

Chapter 40
A Job Offer

They both were startled by the phone ringing. They would have to get used to that right away. Jesse answered the phone. It was an office calling about a position for Bill.

Jesse said, "It's for you, Bill."

Bill took the phone offered by Jesse. The following conversation was heartening. That guy seemed to have been impressed by his re'sume'. Bill was both surprised and pleased about the call. He needed to set a time for an interview. He suggested ten o'clock on Monday morning. That was agreeable to both parties. He quickly made a note about the time.

Jesse got up, took Bill's hand, and congratulated him heartily. "Bill, I believe we both will be employed very soon, don't you?"

They were both on their feet so they decided to put the mail away and see if there were some things they could do around the house that would fill some time for them and make a real home for them and their wives.

After checking on the condition of things inside and finding nothing there really needed their attention, the went outside and found that a bunch of things could be done to improve things out there, but they would need some basic tools to get those jobs done done. Shopping would be in order.

That took a bit of conversation. They really shared the same responsibilities with the yard work. The front lawn was not really large, but with no tools, it would be a challenge. Bill asked, "How can we do this and be fair to everybody concerned?"

Jesse had apparently not put much thought into that aspect of their joint ownership of their new home. He asked, "Do you think we should buy the necessary tools now with you owning some and me owning some. We are here together now but we don't really know how long it will be before that might change."

Bill suggested, "Let's make a list of needed items. Then we can decide about who will buy what."

Jesse wouldn't necessarily need a list, but he agreed that that would be the way to help them decide. Bill went to the car to get a note pad and pen. Jesse was busy making a list in his head. Soon they had it on paper, too. A mower, rake, hedge trimmer, shovel, and some gloves were listed. They got into the car and went to the nearest hardware store. It was a Home Depot. They shopped around, compared makes and prices of lawnmowers. They decided on a self propelled mower. It cost over $200. Then they priced all the other items on the list. They also found some other items they'd need. That was also about $200. That made it easy to decide who would own what.

Jesse said, "That was sort of fun, our shopping for necessities and finding how easy it was to make the purchases."

Bill added, "We really have been sharing our way for two years. I suppose that the girl's idea about our making the same sort of decisions have become a way of life."

When they got home with all of those things plus gas and oil for the mower and hedge trimmer, they were all set to do yard work.

They had really done a good job. All they now needed to do to complete the job, was to sweep the porches, walkways, the drive way, and then to put the tools away.

Chapter 41
And Now a Storage Shed

There was a two car carport attached to both ends of the house, but no storage space that could be under lock and key. Neither of them had considered that necessity. Jesse was busily designing a storage space in his head. Bill did his design on the note paper they had used for their shopping. When Bill showed Jesse his idea on paper, Jesse wasn't surprised that it was almost exactly what he had had in mind.

"Bill, it is really getting uncanny as to how we do have the same thoughts so much of the time. Maybe that is why we get on so well together." Jesse mused.

Bill added, "You know, that is right, but how will we manage getting that constructed this weekend?"

"Maybe there will be a lumber supplier open somewhere. Let's go check that in the phone book." Jesse suggested.

They neatly arranged the tools behind the house near the back doors before going inside. Bill picked up the phone book. The phone rang again. Jesse answered. It was Meg and Jean calling. They had good news. They would be home earlier than they expected on Sunday. He told them about their activities and all of the work they had accomplished. He handed the phone to Bill so he could speak to Jean. It was good to hear from their wives and especially good to hear they would be home earlier than expected.

The girls said they looked forward to seeing the make over of the lawn. All of them would have liked to prolong their visit but the girls were being urged to hurry, so they said their goodbyes.

Jesse had found a source for getting their lumber but when they called, they were told that they would have to wait until Monday before they could get service there.

Bill was checking the want ads. He had found someone who had had some building materials left over after their house was built. They called and found that that just might be what they were looking for. They got directions and were welcomed to come now to see about buying from the owner of the ad.

When they got to that house, the owner was anxious to sell lumber, and other things they would need. It was a good thing that they had brought the trailer. The fellow was so eager to rid himself of his wares, that they got them almost for free.

They took most of what he had on hand and then headed for home. They decided that they perhaps could finish the design tonight, but would building it on Sunday be a good idea? They really were in a very calm subdivision where all the neighbors were friendly, but they were nervous about doing construction work on Sunday. They thought perhaps they would have to wait and see. They checked the time and thought about how hungry they were, They found their meal in the refrigerator and enjoyed every bite before falling into their beds for the night.

Their Sundays with Meg and Jean had been filled with church, eating out and then doing things that they all enjoyed. When morning came, Bill and Jesse were up and ready for the day sort of early. They went for a walk after breakfast in their neighborhood. They were trying to learn what sort of activities were acceptable on Sunday in that part of town.

At first, they didn't see any kind of activity, but soon they found a fellow working on his car. Then they found someone else, pulling some weeds out of a flower bed. All of that was very quietly done. No one was making any noises like sawing and hammering. They spoke to some of the neighbors before returning home.

They decided to combine both of their ideas for the storage unit, and get them on paper. That way, they would be ready to start building when the time was right. The plan took shape rapidly. Bill was doing the pencil work while Jesse was comparing his thought to Bill's drawing. The finished drawing included the best of each man's ideas. Both were satisfied.

They turned on the television and settled down to watch the news. Right away, there was some news about the girl's troupe and how successfully their tour was going. There was even a short blip of Jean and Meg doing a duet on stage. They could still sing as beautifully as ever. After surfing several channels and not finding anything to their liking, they decided to read the mail again.

Their mail was not very neatly arranged, but they reread all of it again anyway. When Bill got to the letter from the same people who had made an appointment for an interview, he saw something he had not noticed before. He said, "Now hear this." Jesse looked his way as Bill started reading. Bill read, 'We really have two openings in that department.'

"Jesse, they might have a job you would like." said Bill.

Jesse said, "Don't you remember we sent most of our re'sume's to the same places.

They know where I am, also."

He had hardly finished speaking when the phone rang again. Bill answered this time. He handed Jesse the phone. Jesse asked, "Who is it?"

Bill said, "Just answer it."

Bill thought he had heard that voice on the phone recently. Sure enough. It was the same fellow calling for an appointment for Jesse. Of course Jesse accepted and said they would come together as there was only one car available when their wives were working.

That led to a little celebratory gig all around the room. Things were definitely looking better for all of them.

They were wishing that they had a phone number to use to phone Meg and Jean but they did not have one. They decided time might go by a bit faster if they just got some sleep. When they were in bed a few minutes, the phone rang again.

It was Meg. She had forgotten if she had told them that she and Jean would be home all next week until Friday. They would be starting a new series of programs the following week which would take them out of town once in a while. They were getting home tomorrow night.

All of that was good news, and when Jesse said he and Bill had appointments for interviews on Monday, the girls squealed loudly and giggled and went completely haywire. Soon they said good-night. They were almost as wildly giddy as the girls had been. They couldn't go to sleep so they got up to hear the late news.

The girls would soon be home. They loved to plan things for them that would let them know how much they were loved. Perhaps they could get the storage shed completed before they arrived.

Chapter 42
Working Together

They wakened early and quickly had a coffee before they got out the tools and wood for the shed. Their plan was to build it across the back of the one of the car ports. They would start by building a wall across the back of theparking spaces. Then they would actually build two enclosures. One would be deeper and house the mower, hedge trimmer and other big tools. It would be locked up tight. The other would store the smaller pieces behind locked doors . They were expecting their wives any minute, so they were hurrying to finish and get cleaned up before they arrived.

They did get finished and had almost gotten all the tools in the shed before the girls drove in. They were pleasantly surprised and pleased that the end result was attractive and useful, too.

The newly weds had just had their first separation from each other this weekend. All were glad that that was over and now things could get back to normal, whatever that was? They had moved mountains in the first two weeks of married bliss. Jean and Meg had started their new jobs after returning from four days at Atlantic Beach, They had moved their worldly goods from school to Asheville, and had bought a duplex for both couples to live in side by side. It was as if all their dreams had come true at once.

The guys told the girls about their upcoming interview tomorrow at ten o'clock. Then they had to tell the whole news about the storage shed construction. That way we would be here when you two got home. And here we are, all together again."

Jean wanted to know what the job was and what the company was. The guys were glad to tell it all.

Bill began by saying, "You have heard about the North Carolina Department of Transportation, commonly called the DOT. They want two engineers to work right here in western North Carolina on redesigning some of the trouble spots along the interstates."

Meg asked, "What is wrong with the interstates?"

"There have been some problems from time to time ever since they were first built. Heretofore, they just fixed the new problem and went on about their business. Now there is a movement afoot to get all those trouble spots corrected alike as soon as possible. We will design the improvements for those that lay on the horizon." Bill answered and then said, "Jesse, do you have anything to add to my explanation/"

"Yes, but you have about said it all. I just want to add that they are looking for newly trained first class engineers in order to get a new prospective on these problems. I suppose Bill and I must have had the proper attributes to get their attention. Now Meg my dear, it is time for us to go home and get filled in on all of your doings and get out of Bill's and Jean's way so that they can do the same."

Jean added, "We are so very glad to get back home to this cozy little house and find our men to have had a busy and useful weekend with yard work and construction. Our homes are getting nearer to being perfect all the time."

Meg asked, "Do you think you will receive a definitive answer tomorrow about your work?"

"That of course remains to be seen, but I feel that the DOT does not make many offers that they do not feel really good about. I just hope we will be hired and be able to work together, don't you Bill?" Jesse asked.

"You bet. Now you folk go home so we can get back to that togetherness business."

Jesse and Meg flew out the door. Jean fell into Bill's arms and cuddled as of old.

It was sort of like starting their honeymoon all over again but in a different environment that they would continue to live in for an indefinite length of time and call it home.

Tuesday dawned bright and early. The appointment was at ten so they got right to the business of breakfast and dressing suitably for such an occasion. The girls saw them both off and then sat down together in the carport to visit and make plans for the coming days.

Chapter 43
In the Newspaper?

They were pleasantly surprised when two of their neighbors stopped in to visit. They started by remarking about the industriousness of their husbands. They were complimentary as to the lawn and the new shed. The girls were pleased to have them saying all those good things about their husbands.

Jean asked, "They didn't disturb anyone with their building, did they?"

"Oh, my no. We all have a loud bit of work to do sometimes. My husband was particularly interested in the design and the ease with which they got it all together."

Jean explained, "They have just graduated with degrees in engineering and this is their first joint venture. They are now being interviewed by the DOT for jobs in their field."

"Do you mean right at this minute?" One neighbor asked.

Meg added, "Yes, that is correct and we just can't wait to hear the outcome. We have been away on a weekend tour with the 'Voices of Harmony' troupe. We do not have to go in today until seven tonight when we will be performing at the Civic Center.

Jean and I both sing with that group at this time."

"Wonderful. We are planning to go to that performance. This is the first time we will know some of the performers. What do you each do?"

Jean explained, "We have been best friends since third grade in Murphy, we have all just graduated from WCU and gotten married. We are just home from our honeymoon and have gotten settled in and are pretty much ready for anything that comes our way."

"What a happy story that would make! I am a contributor to the local news papers. Could I write about you folk having just moved here and are already involved in so many things.?"

Jean and Meg were surprised that she thought that our moving here and doing our work here, was newsworthy. Too, neither of them had really learned their guests names.

Meg asked, "We were sort of surprised to be receiving guests today. However we are very glad to have our neighbors visit and get acquainted. When we have been home, we were totally involved in getting our house livable before we left for the weekend. We would like to learn your names and you to learn ours and perhaps we can become really good friends."

"Oh, yes. We want that also. Most of the people in this section are friendly and all get along well together. Some have become best friends with each other. Is that how you ladies feel about being neighborly?"

The tallest and blondest lady said, "Why don't we learn each others names, like they asked of us and then let these ladies get settled in after being away? I am Loretta Hughs. I live across the street at 243 Lakeview. This is Mary Lou Simms. She lives next door to me at 245 Lakeview. Our husbands are Jim and Eddy. We each have children. May and Josephine are my two girls. Mary Lou has two boys and a girl. They are preschool. Their names are Larry and Terrance and the baby is Julie."

Mary Lou asked, "Loretta, don't you think we had best get along home before the 'baby sitters' send out a posse to track us down?"

Jean said, "We are so very glad to get to know some new neighbors. And yes, you may write all the articles you want about us. I think you will have to have them approved by us and our employers before printing them in the news. Oh, and by the way, I am Jean Buckner Davis and She is Meg Turner Ray. Our husbands names are Bill and Jesse. And do feel welcome anytime we are here."

Loretta asked, "Are you sure? I need your approval of the printed message before I can have it published in the hometown newspaper? And I also need the approval of the Voices of Harmony troupe?

"Yes, that is right"

"But that isn't even standard procedure." Loretta explained"Articles for the newspaper are syndicated. If it is news, we print it."

"We have just started singing with this group. I do not want anything to mar our image or to upset our employers.." stressed Jean.

Meg had heard both Loretta and Jean, but she just couldn't believe that she was hearing discord with their new neighbors. Meg tried to explain, "Loretta, Jean is exhausted with our weekend tour and just isn't thinking right. Let's talk about it more tomorrow when our husbands are here."

Loretta was not one to upset people. And in her work, she usually didn't get asked to get approval before printing news worthy news. She said before taking her leave, "I am sorry to have upset anyone. Do forgive my attitude."

Jean responded to her apology by saying, "Our fathers are the Mayor and City Manager in Murphy. We have grown up with the idea that any news to be printed about our family members , had to be approved before it went to press. I feel sure that you and your paper will find that a policy to be worthy of following."

The neighbors left with a brief wave, goodby.

After the neighbors left, Jean and Meg went indoors. They were both aware of that long lasting regulation concerning newspaper articles about their families. Both girls sat and thought a bit before discussing that exchange in their yard.

Meg spoke first. "Jean, I know that we have the right to say what we think is right, and I am glad that you spoke up. There is no telling what people might conger up about us and our work. Please don't be upset about it."

Jean didn't answer immediately. When she spoke, she sounded normal, which was a very good sign. "I just hope what we say and do doesn't have any bad effects on our daily lives. Now let's forget that and get in the kitchen an get normal."

Chapter 44
Engineering for the DOT

When Bill and Jesse returned, they pretended that their news wasn't good at first. The girls soon got the real story. Their husbands were both employed by the NC DOT. The girls had a great meal prepared to celebrate their good news. Afterwards, they told them about their neighbor's visit.

The good news far out shown the news the girls were sharing. Both men were upset about all that news. They were quietly thinking just how they should react, if indeed they did react.

Their thoughts were interrupted by a knock on the door. Jesse answered the door. There were a couple of neighbors on their doorstep.

When Jean heard the woman's voice, she thought it must be Loretta. She joined Jesse at the door. They invited them inside and after all were seated, Loretta's husband spoke. He seemed to be a bit tense. Bill asked, "Are you the neighbors from across the street who called earlier today?"

Jim answered, "Yes. We want to make amends and get off to a good start with our new neighbors. My wife, Loretta, has told me that she was surprised to learn that you folk were already engaged in so much in our town within such a short time. She thought that all of that was newsworthy. She also said she was surprised to hear Jean tell her that her article about you people would need to receive your personal approval before publication." He paused before going on.

Jesse interrupted, "Yes. That is how that usually works in places we have lived heretofore. Bill and I have just been signed up as new engineers for the North Carolina Department of Transportation. Did you read about my graduating Magnum Cum Laude with only two and a half years instead of the four years usually required to complete that engineering course at WCU? I am not bragging. I just think all of us have accomplished a lot in our few years on earth. The rest took the whole four years and enjoyed all of it. Now we are all ready to get on with our adult lives and get along with all our new neighbors, too."

Loretta just couldn't be quiet any longer. She said, "I have never before heard of anyone accomplishing what you have accomplished. How did you do it?"

Chapter 45
More Memory Problems

Meg, too, could not keep quiet any longer. "My husband is gifted with a photographic memory. He did all that without taking notes or reading his textbooks more than once. We are not bragging, just stating the facts."

Bill spoke up, "You have no idea how difficult it has been for us to try to understand Jesse's gift. He doesn't flaunt it. He was born with it and he has to live with it. It is a very handy blessing."

Loretta asked, "Can you explain just how a photographic memory works?"

"Of course, up to a point. It is an inherited characteristic that is handed down in families by a particular gene. Only the children who are born with it are capable of passing it on. No one can learn how to do it. You either have it, or you don't. I can repeat all of our conversation verbatim, if you would care to hear it."

Loretta wanted to contest him on that. She asked Jesse to repeat the words of her husband when he first spoke after being seated.

Jesse repeated, "Yes. We want to make amends and get off to a good start with our new neighbors. My wife, Loretta, has told me that she was surprised to learn that you folk were already engaged in so much in our town within such a short time. She thought that all of that was newsworthy. She also said she was surprised to hear Jean tell her that her article about you people would have to receive your personal approval before publication."

The guests were speechless after his recitation. The foursome were not surprised at all, but they too, had never heard him perform that particular feat.

Bill asked, "How much of our interview can you recite?"

Jesse said, "All of it. I can do it now or next week sometime. Which way shall it be?"

Bill threw up his arms and said, "I thought that I had experienced all of your talent in some form or other, but now I know that is not so."

Their guests were thoughtfully trying to comprehend just what Jesse had done.

Jesse came to their aid, "I promise that I will keep this bad habit I have under wraps most of the time. Otherwise, I might be put in a side show at the circus just like my Mother has told me about in the past."

Jim asked, " Are there any downsides to your ability?"

"Yes, sir. I keep remembering all of the sad and unhappy things I have observed in my life. When I served in Iraq, I saw many of my comrades fall from injuries or death. I can't get that out of my head, either."

Loretta observed, "How is it that four such talented people got together, got educated, got married, and got involved in such interesting occupations?"

"We attribute that to a lot of good luck. The first of which was when Jean and Meg first met. They were at school on opening day when Jean's family had just moved to Murphy. Meg was in her third grade classroom alone awaiting the arrival of her teacher. Jean and her parents entered the room and Meg offered to assist them if she could. They asked where the teacher was. Meg told them she would be there any minute. She arrived and while the parents and teacher conferred, Meg asked Jean to come to sit beside her. They have been friends ever since." Bill explained.

Meg said, "Our meeting Jesse was somewhat like that. Jean and I had rented a house at the edge of the campus for our first two years in college. We were throwing a party for two friends for their birthdays the day before classes began in our Junior year. We had cleaned and decorated our porch with potted plants brought from home. During the night, someone had dumped out the pots, turned over the furniture and broken the table. We were trying to get it all cleaned up when we heard footsteps on our driveway. It was a young man that we had not known before. He offered to help us reset the plants. He did it so deftly, that we added him to our guest list and for him arrive at five that afternoon. We have been friends ever since. Bill was already one of Jean's dates during our sophomore year."

"I so want to write all this for the newspaper. How about it?" Loretta asked.

Jim added, "It all is so very interesting and unusual. Are there any parts that you have left off?"

Jean said, "I hope you are not finding us conceited about our gifts. Both of these fellows are gifted in other ways. Bill is an artist. Jesse is a poet. They have earned the money we are using to get settled in this house by using their talents. Meg and I have always sung together or apart since childhood. Now we are singing with the local traveling troupe, 'The Voices of Harmony.'. I hope that you will be able to continue to enjoy that group when we perform in this area."

"I have never met any folk just like you, one at a time or in bunches as you are now. What can we do to make up for any trouble we have caused thus far?" Jim asked.

Jesse spoke for his foursome, "We just want to live and let live and come to be good neighbors for as long as we are fortunate enough to be here among you good people."

Loretta jumped to her feet, saying "I am so glad to hear you want us to start our relationship all over again. We, too, will work hard to accept all that you have told us and to be good neighbors."

Everyone got on their feet. They shook hands and visited a bit more before the guests left.

"Whew, that was some visit. I hope all can be worked out over time. How do the rest of you feel about it?" Jesse asked.

"We are all in this together. May we be able to fit in respectfully enough for all concerned." Bill said. Then he added, "And that they all do likewise."

Jean spoke from the heart, "I think we are still riding off into the sunset just as we did when we left WCU to go on our honeymoons."

"And let that be a lesson for us all. We are still learning to fit into this big wide world and may we continue to do it gracefully as we have in the past." Jesse summed it all up.

9 781466 364554